Misha ... ary

Simple Perfection

ALSO BY ABBI GLINES

The *Perfection* series
Twisted Perfection
Simple Perfection

The *Too Far* series
Fallen Too Far
Never Too Far
Forever Too Far

The *Sea Breeze* series
Breathe
Because of Low
While It Lasts
Just for Now

The *Vincent Boys* series
The Vincent Boys
The Vincent Brothers

The *Existence* series
Existence
Predestined
Ceaseless

Simple
Perfection

A Novel

Abbi Glines

ATRIA PAPERBACK

New York • London • Toronto • Sydney • New Delhi

ATRIA PAPERBACK
A Division of Simon & Schuster, Inc.
1230 Avenue of the Americas
New York, NY 10020

First Atria Paperback edition December 2013

ATRIA PAPERBACK and colophon are trademarks of Simon & Schuster, Inc.

For information about special discounts for bulk purchases, please contact Simon & Schuster Special Sales at 1-866-506-1949 or business@simonandschuster.com.

The Simon & Schuster Speakers Bureau can bring authors to your live event. For more information or to book an event, contact the Simon & Schuster Speakers Bureau at 1-866-248-3049 or visit our website at www.simonspeakers.com.

Interior design by Dana Sloan

Manufactured in the United States of America

10 9 8 7 6 5 4 3 2

Library of Congress Cataloging-in-Publication Data is available.

ISBN 978-1-4767-5652-3
ISBN 978-1-4767-5653-0 (ebook)

To my husband, Keith.
Thanks for being my safe place.

Acknowledgments

When I decided to write about Woods I hadn't yet envisioned Della. But once I started writing her, wow. I fell in love. It takes more than just me and a MacBook to get a story written, though.

I need to start by thanking my agent, Jane Dystel, who is beyond brilliant. Signing with her was one of the smartest things I've ever done. Thank you, Jane, for helping me navigate through the waters of the publishing world. You are truly a badass.

When I signed with Atria I was lucky enough to be given Jhanteigh Kupihea as my editor. She is always positive and working to make my books the best they can be. Thank you, Jhanteigh, for making my new life with Atria one I am happy to be a part of. The rest of the Atria team: Judith Curr for giving me and my books a chance. Ariele Fredman and Valerie Vennix for always finding the best marketing ideas and being as awesome as they are brilliant.

The friends who listen to me and understand me the way no one else in my life can: Colleen Hoover, Jamie McGuire, and Tammara Webber. You three have listened to me and supported me more than anyone I know. Thanks for everything.

When I finished *Simple Perfection*, I was worried about the major twists I knew no one was expecting. I wanted to know how readers would react. These two ladies always drop what they are doing to read my manuscripts and tell me their honest opinions. I cherish that. Thank you Autumn Hull and Natasha Tomic for being my eager readers and never holding back a punch.

Last but certainly not least:

My family. Without their support I wouldn't be here. My husband, Keith, makes sure I have my coffee and the kids are all taken care of when I need to lock myself away and meet a deadline. My three kids are so understanding, although once I walk out of that writing cave they expect my full attention and they get it. My parents, who have supported me all along. Even when I decided to write steamier stuff. My friends, who don't hate me because I can't spend time with them for weeks at a time because my writing is taking over. They are my ultimate support group and I love them dearly.

My readers. I never expected to have so many of you. Thank you for reading my books. For loving them and telling others about them. Without you I wouldn't be here. It's that simple.

Simple Perfection

Woods

My mother hadn't spoken to me during my father's funeral. I had gone to comfort her but she turned from me and walked away. There were a lot of things I expected in life, but that hadn't been one of them. Ever. Nothing that I'd done had affected my mother's life. However, she'd helped my father as he had tried to destroy mine.

Seeing him lying there cold and still in the casket hadn't struck me the way I imagined. Everything was too fresh. I hadn't had time to forgive him. He had hurt Della. I could never forgive that. Even with him dead and buried in the ground I couldn't forgive what he'd done to her. She was the center of my world.

My mother had been able to see the lack of emotion in my eyes. I wasn't one for pretending. At least not anymore. A week ago I had walked away from this life I'd been born into without one ounce of remorse. It hadn't been hard to let it all go. My focus had been on finding Della. The woman who had walked into my life and changed everything. Della Sloane had become my addiction when I hadn't been available. In all her twisted perfection she had made me fall helplessly in love with her. A life without her in it seemed pointless. I often wondered how people found joy in life without knowing her.

1

With the sudden death of my father, the life I had just washed my hands of and been so ready to walk away from was now being placed completely on my shoulders. Della had stood beside me quietly from the moment I'd stepped foot back in Rosemary Beach, Florida. Her small hand tucked into mine, she knew when I needed her without my saying anything. A squeeze from her hand would remind me that she was there beside me and I could do this.

Except at this moment she wasn't with me. She was at my house. I hadn't wanted to bring her here, to my mother's house. My mother might have wanted to pretend that I didn't exist but I now owned everything in her life, including the house she lived in. It came with the country club, and my grandfather had made sure that when my father passed away this would all become mine.

Not once had my father thought this might be something I needed to know. He held it over my head that he controlled my life. If I wanted this world, then I had to bend to his will. Yet all along it would become mine on my twenty-fifth birthday or in the event of my father's death. Whichever came first. There was no running from this now.

I thought about knocking and changed my mind. My mother needed to stop acting like a child. I was all she had left. It was time she accepted Della in my life, because I was getting a ring on her finger as soon as I could convince her of it. I knew Della well enough to know that it wouldn't be easy to get her to marry me. With my world completely morphing into something I hadn't expected, I wanted the security of knowing that when I came home Della would be there.

I started to reach for the doorknob when the door swung

open. My eyes lifted to see Angelina Greystone standing in the doorway of my parents' house with an innocent smile on her face. The evil twinkle in her eye couldn't be masked by her attempt to appear nice. I had almost married this woman so that I could get the club that was going to become mine anyway. My father had made me believe I had to marry Angelina to get the promotion and future I deserved.

What my dad hadn't banked on was Della walking into my life and showing me there was more for me than a loveless marriage to a heartless bitch.

"We were expecting you. Your mother is in the sitting room with some chamomile tea I made for her. She needs to see you, Woods. I'm glad you took her feelings into consideration and didn't bring that girl."

The one thing I did know, despite what the witch had just said, was she knew Della's name. She might have wanted to pretend like she had never heard of her and didn't know her, but she did. She was just being spiteful. What I didn't know was why the fuck she was at my mother's house.

I pushed past her and walked into the house without responding to her. I knew where my mother was without her help. The sitting room was the place my mother always went to be alone. She would sit on the white velvet chaise lounge that had once been my grandmother's and she would stare out at the water through the large picture windows that lined the room.

I ignored the click of Angelina's heels as she followed behind me. Everything about her grated on my nerves. Her being here in the middle of a family situation on the day of my father's funeral only added to my disgust. Why was she doing this? What did she think this would win her? I owned it all now. Me. Not my father. And certainly not my mother. I was now the Kerrington in control.

"Mother," I said as I walked into the sitting room without knocking. She didn't need a chance to send me away. Not that I would go without having this conversation. As wrong as she had been, I loved her. She was my mom, even though she had always stood beside my father and never once thought of me. It had always been about what they wanted for me. But it didn't make me love her less.

She didn't turn her attention from the gulf view outside. "Woods, I was expecting you." Nothing more. It hurt. We had both lost a part of our lives with my father's death. She didn't see it that way. She never would.

I walked over to stand in her line of view. "We need to talk," I replied simply.

She shifted her eyes to look up at me. "Yes, we do."

I could have let her control this conversation but I wasn't going to. It was time I set some boundaries. Especially now that I had Della with me and we were back in Rosemary.

"At least he came alone." Angelina's voice came from the door and I jerked my head to glare at her intrusion. She wasn't a part of this.

"This doesn't concern you. You may leave," I replied in a cold tone.

She flinched.

"She is a part of this. She's going to stay with me. I need someone here so I'm not alone and Angelina understands that. She's a good girl. She would have made an excellent daughter-in-law."

I understood my mother's pain at losing my father was

fresh—and she *was* in pain. But I wouldn't let her control this. It was time I made some things very clear for both of them. "She would have been a selfish spoiled bitch of a daughter-in-law. I was lucky enough to realize it before it was too late and I ruined my life." I heard both of their sharp intakes of breath but I wasn't about to let them speak. "I control everything now, Mother. I will take care of you. I will make sure you want for nothing. However, I will not accept or acknowledge Angelina in my life. More importantly, I will not allow anyone to hurt Della. I will protect her from both of you. She is my perfection. She holds my heart in her hands. When she hurts it brings me to my knees. There is no way to explain to you the way I feel about her. Just understand that I will not allow anyone to hurt her again. I won't forgive that. I lose a piece of my soul when I see her in pain."

The tight line of my mother's mouth was the only answer I needed. She wasn't accepting this. Today wasn't the day to try to convince her about my feelings for Della. She was mourning and I was still angry with the man she was mourning. "If you need anything, call me. When you're ready to talk to me without resentment toward Della, then call me. We will talk. You're my mother and I love you. But I won't let you near Della, nor will I put you before her. Understand that if you make me choose, I will choose her without a second thought."

I walked over and placed a kiss on the top of my mother's head before walking past Angelina without a word. It was time I got back home. Della didn't do well alone. I was always anxious when I left her.

Della

He still hadn't cried. No emotion at all. I hated that. I wanted him to grieve. He needed to let it out instead of bottling his emotions because of me. The idea that he was hardened toward his pain because he was protecting me twisted my gut. His father had betrayed him by sending me away. But I had seen the look in Woods's eyes as he looked at his father, seeking approval. He had loved his father. He needed to mourn his loss.

"Della?" I turned to see Woods walk into the living room. His eyes scanned the room before they found me standing outside on the balcony. He immediately headed for the door. There was a determination in his eyes that worried me. He opened the door and stepped outside.

"Hey, did things go okay?" I asked before he pulled me into his arms and held me tightly against him. He had done this a lot over the past week.

"She's grieving. We will talk again once she's had time to process everything," he said into my hair. "I missed you."

I smiled sadly and pulled back so I could look up at him. "You were gone for about an hour. Not much time to miss me."

Woods ran his hand through my hair, brushing it out of

the way, and then cupped my face. "I missed you the second I walked out that door. I want you with me all the time."

Smiling, I turned my head and kissed his hand. "I can't always be with you."

Woods's eyes darkened with something I recognized well. "But I want you with me." He slipped one of his arms around my waist, tugging me up against him. "I can't concentrate when I'm not close enough to touch you."

I grinned as I pressed a kiss to the inside of his wrist. "When you touch me we tend to get carried away."

Woods's hand slipped under my shirt and I shivered as he moved it closer to my chest. "Right now I want to get carried away."

I wanted that too. I always wanted that, but he needed to talk. He needed to say something.

His phone rang, interrupting both of us.

His face tensed and he let his hand slide out from underneath my shirt reluctantly before reaching into his pocket to pull out his phone.

"Hello," he said in his business tone. He looked at me apologetically. "Yeah, I'll be there in five minutes. Tell him to meet me in my dad's . . . in my office."

He was having a hard time calling his dad's office "his." That was only another glimpse into the pain he was ignoring.

"That was Vince. There are several board members in town and they want to meet with me in an hour. Gary, my dad's adviser and best friend, wants to brief me first. I'm sorry," he said, reaching out to take my hand and pull me against him.

"Don't be sorry. There is nothing to be sorry about. If there's anything I can do to help you, then I will. Just tell me."

Woods chuckled. "If I could get away with keeping you in my office all day with me, then I would."

"Hmmm . . . I don't think you'd get a lot of work done."

"I know I wouldn't," he replied.

"Go, show that board that you're ready for this."

Woods pressed a kiss to my head. "What are you going to do?"

I wanted to work again. I missed seeing everyone and having something to do. Lying on the beach every day wasn't really me. "Could I have my job back?" I asked.

A frown wrinkled Woods's brow. "No. I don't want you working in the dining room."

I had been prepared for this. "Okay. Then I'm going to go find a job somewhere else. I need something to do. Especially with you being so busy."

"What if you need me? Where would you want to work? What if I can't get to you? That won't work, Della. I can't protect you if you aren't near me." I was only adding more stress for him. He needed more time to adjust. I would give him that. He needed to heal. I would have to find a way to spend my days.

"Okay. We'll wait a couple weeks and talk about it again," I said with a smile, hoping to reassure him.

He looked relieved. That was what I had wanted. "I'll call you once this meeting is over. We'll have dinner together. I won't leave you here alone long. I swear."

I just nodded.

Woods pulled me to him and kissed me. It was a possessive kiss. Right now he needed me to be there for him. For now, that is what I would do. Be there for him.

"I love you," he whispered against my lips, and then pressed one last kiss to them.

"I love you, too," I replied.

◇

Woods left and I stayed outside on the balcony looking out at the gulf. I had missed out on life for so long and now I was learning that life was about sacrifice. Especially when you loved someone.

My phone rang this time and I picked it up from the table I'd left it on earlier. It was an unknown number. That meant one thing: it was Tripp.

"Hey," I said, sitting down on the lounge chair beside me.

"How are things?"

"Okay. Woods is adjusting," I replied.

Tripp let out a weary sigh. "I should've come home for the funeral. I just . . . I couldn't."

I didn't know what it was in Rosemary that haunted Tripp. But I knew that something did. Since he'd left he had called me twice. Both times it had been from an unknown number and both times he had seemed off. Almost depressed.

"Jace said he tried to get in contact with you and couldn't. You've changed your number."

"Yeah. I did. I needed some space."

"Jace misses you. He worries about you."

Tripp didn't respond and I didn't feel like I was the person who should push him to respond.

"I'll call him. Let him know there's no reason to worry. I shouldn't have stayed in Rosemary so long. It messes with my head. I can't go back there. There're things . . . stuff I don't like to face."

I already knew this. I had no idea what those things were but I knew that they haunted him.

"Are you working again?" he asked.

"No. Woods doesn't want me working right now. He needs me to be available for him. I'm his only source of support. His mother . . . well . . . you know how she is."

Tripp paused a moment and I wondered what he was thinking about. I really didn't want him to say something negative about Woods. "Right now he needs you. I get it. But, Della, you started this journey to live life. Don't forget that. You left one prison; don't find yourself in another."

His words sliced through me painfully. Woods was nothing like my mother. He needed me right now because he had lost his father and been thrown into a position he wasn't prepared for overnight. He wasn't trying to control me. "This is different. I'm choosing to stand beside Woods. I love him and I will be here for whatever he needs. Once he's better he'll be fine with me getting a job again."

Tripp didn't respond and we sat there for a few minutes in silence. I wondered if he disagreed or if he wasn't sure what to say to that.

"The next time I call I won't block my number. I want you to have it if you need it."

I wouldn't need his number.

"Just . . . don't give it to Jace or anyone. Please."

"Good-bye, Tripp," I replied before ending the call. I didn't want to hear his doubt and concern. He was wrong. Everything was going to be fine with Woods and me. He was very wrong.

One month later

Woods

I glanced over at the phone and considered calling Della. I hadn't spoken to her in five hours. My morning had been packed with meetings and conference calls. She never complained. That bothered me. The fact was I thought she should complain. I was failing her. How was I supposed to run the Kerrington Club and take care of her? Any other woman would have been in my office throwing a fit. But never Della.

A swift knock on my door kept me from picking up the phone. I would call her in a minute. "Come in," I called out, and started looking for the papers Vince had brought me to sign earlier.

"Vince wasn't out there so I knocked." Angelina's voice wasn't what I expected to hear.

"What does Mother need now?" I asked without looking up at her. That was why she was here. At first I had been annoyed with her presence but she was helping my mother more than I could. More than I wanted to.

"She misses you. It's been over a week since you called to check on her."

Angelina was as good at guilt trips as my mother was. The

two of them were so much alike. "I'll call her later today. I've got work. If that's all, please see yourself out."

"You don't have to treat me so coldly. I'm helping you the only way I know how. Every day I stay here with your mother is for you. It's all for you. I'm in love with you, Woods. I can't compete for your heart because you won't allow me in. But what is she doing for you? I don't see her helping you—"

"Enough. Don't ever put yourself on the same level as Della. I didn't ask you to take care of my mother. I can hire someone to help me if I need it. As for Della, she's the reason I get out of bed each morning, so never underestimate her importance."

Angelina stiffened and opened her mouth to say more. I lowered my angry glare back to the contracts in front of me. I was done with this conversation. "Leave."

The clicking of her heels on the hardwood floors as she left the office was the most welcome sound I'd heard all day.

When the door closed behind her I reached for my phone to call Della.

"Hello," her sweet voice said into the phone.

"I need you," I replied.

"I just finished a late lunch with Blaire and Bethy. I'll be right there," she replied.

"Just come in when you get here," I told her.

"Okay."

⊠

Exactly ten minutes and fifteen seconds later my door opened and Della stepped inside. Her dark hair was pulled up into a ponytail. The short sundress she was wearing hugged her curves more than I would have preferred. I stood up and walked around my desk.

"Hi," she said with a shy smile.

"Hi," I replied before resting both my hands on her hips and pressing my mouth on hers. Her lips were always so plump and soft. The faint taste of cherries from her lip gloss clung to my tongue.

This was what I needed. This was what got me through each day.

Della broke the kiss and placed her hands on either side of my face. "Are you okay?" she asked softly.

"I am now."

Della gazed up at me as if she were studying me closely. Then she stepped back and turned to the door. Before I could ask her what she was doing the lock clicked in place.

"Take off your clothes," she said simply, then began to slip the straps of her dress down her shoulders.

I was at a loss for words at the moment. I did as I was told. I couldn't take my eyes off of Della. As her dress pooled at her feet and she stood there in nothing but a pair of pink lace panties and a matching bra, my hands started to tremble. Seeing her like this never got old.

"We haven't made love in here yet," she said, smiling at me as she unsnapped her bra and let it drop carelessly to the floor.

"No we haven't," I managed to say. When she hooked her fingers in the sides of her panties and started pulling them down, I reached my breaking point. The moment she stepped out of the pink lace I took the two steps separating us and picked her up, and her legs wrapped firmly around me. You couldn't call what our mouths were doing kissing. It was too raw for that. We were taking each other. It was the best description I could think of.

I wanted to take her on my desk but we weren't going to

make it that far. Not after that striptease. I wasn't even going to be able to enjoy tasting her and touching her. I needed to be inside her now before I exploded.

I set her down and flipped her around until she was facing the wall. "Brace yourself," I whispered into her ear.

Della leaned forward and placed both her hands against the wall. I took in the sight of her body arched out and my heart slammed against my chest. She was beautiful. Perfect. Grabbing her by the hips, I sank inside of her. The cry of pleasure was so loud I was pretty damn sure Vince had heard it outside at his desk, but I didn't care.

"So good, it always feels so good," I whispered in her ear. The shiver that went over her body made me smile.

"Harder," Della panted, pressing her sweet round ass back against me.

I slammed inside of her and stopped. Buried deep, I leaned forward and caressed her breasts. "You make me crazy, baby."

Della only moaned and wiggled her bottom. She wanted me to move.

"It's so tight. You feel like heaven. I want to stay right here for fucking ever," I swore, and I meant it. Della's pussy sucked me like the sweetest mouth I'd ever known.

The tight hole I worshipped squeezed me and I froze. Then she did it again. What the fuck? It was like she was pumping my dick. "Holy shit," I growled. She was gonna make me come way before I wanted to. I slid out of her and back in and the squeezing started again. "Baby, you're gonna make me come," I said in a strangled voice. I was fighting back the heat tightening in my cock. I was so close. "Della, baby, stop doing that. I'm gonna fucking explode. I can't hold back."

She stuck her bottom out farther and the walls of her silky heat squeezed me tighter. It was as if she had just taken the control of my body away from me. I felt myself erupt as I called out her name and my body jerked helplessly against her.

"Yes! Oh God, yes!" Della cried out, and her body went rigid in my arms before it began to shake underneath me. I wrapped both my arms around her and held her as we both came back down from the climax she'd sent us spiraling off into.

"What the hell did you do to me?" I asked, holding her close.

She leaned back against my chest and a smile tugged at her lips. "I fucked you and I did a real good job," she replied.

I hadn't expected that response. Laughing, I picked her up, carried her over to the nearest chair, and sank down into it with her in my arms.

"That was incredible," I told her before pressing a kiss to her neck.

"Do you feel better now?" she asked, arching her neck so I could access it better.

"That depends," I replied.

"On what?"

"If I can convince you to stay in here with me all day."

"You have to work," she said, turning her head to look up at me.

"Mmm, but if you're here with me I can concentrate. And then you can get naked for me again and be a naughty girl when I need you."

Della threw her head back and laughed. The sound of it made everything in my world right.

Della

The phone on Woods's desk beeped twice. "Mr. Kerrington, Miss Greystone is here to see you," the secretary's voice announced through the speaker.

Woods closed his eyes and laid his head back on the chair we were sitting in. "Damn. What the hell does she need now?"

Did she come here often? I fought back the jealousy that wanted to eat its way inside me. Of course she came by to see him. She was staying with his mother and helping her deal with things, which in turn was helping Woods. Unlike me. I wasn't doing anything to help him. I didn't know what to do.

I started to get out of his lap but his hands tightened on me.

"We need to get dressed."

"Don't leave me here with her."

I leaned over and kissed the tip of his nose. "I won't go anywhere. But I prefer to be wearing clothes when she walks in."

Woods let out a sigh and let go of me so I could get up and get dressed.

"You get dressed, too. I don't care what she's seen before me, I don't want her seeing it now."

Woods laughed out loud and stood up. "I'm going to put my clothes on, sexy. Calm down."

We both grinned at each other as we dressed. I liked the idea of her coming in here and seeing us together and knowing what we had been doing. It was silly for me to feel that way, but I did.

"You can send her in," Woods replied, standing at his desk while he watched me fix my hair, which our wild sex had messed up. My ponytail was barely hanging on.

The door swung open and I spun around to see Angelina strutting inside like she belonged here. "I don't know why you . . ." Her voice trailed off as her gaze landed on me. I finished adjusting my ponytail and let my hands fall back down to my sides.

"Did you really just—"

"Why are you back?" Woods cut off her question.

Angelina jerked her gaze to him as if he'd slapped her. I watched as she fought to compose herself. Woods hadn't bothered to run his fingers through his hair and it was messed up from my hands being in it. I bit back a smile as I looked at his properly rumpled appearance.

"I came back to tell you your mother wants to have you over for dinner," Angelina said tightly.

"Unless Della is invited, I'm afraid I won't be able to make it."

Angelina let out a frustrated sigh and shot me an annoyed glance before looking back at Woods. "She's your mother, Woods. She just lost her husband and she's hurting. You're all she has left. Don't you get that? Do you not care?"

She was right. Woods's mother might never like me. But she was his mother, and right now she needed him. "I want you to go, Woods," I said before he could say anything.

He looked over at me and frowned.

"Please," I said, hoping he wouldn't argue with me in front of her.

Woods ran a hand through his hair and I smiled at the way it was still messed up. He was adorable like that. "Fine. But only for an hour. This will also be a one-time thing. Next time I have dinner with her, Della will be with me."

Angelina's annoyed grimace turned into a pleased smile. She would get him tonight, too, without me around. I hated that but I couldn't let it keep Woods from his mother.

"I'm glad you're thinking with something other than your dick," Angelina replied before spinning around and heading out the door.

"She's a bitch. Ignore her," Woods said, shoving off from the desk he'd been leaning on and walking over to me.

"I know," I assured him, but deep down I worried that she was right.

◇

"They're at the door, Della. Don't let them in here. They'll hurt us. All they want to do is hurt us. We have to keep your brother safe. They tried to kill him before. They'll kill us this time. Don't let them in. Shhhh. Stop that crying, you little brat! You have to be quiet. So very quiet, then they'll go away."

I covered my mouth with both my hands to keep in the terrified cries I couldn't control. I hated when this happened. Mom would get mean afterward. She didn't like it when people knocked on our door. It upset her. And she would talk to him. He wasn't there, but she saw him. That scared me, too.

"Get up! They're gone. Go to the door and get the package they left and be careful that they don't see you."

I didn't want to open the door. I wasn't sure what was out there that wanted to get me, but I didn't want to open the door. Momma had been making me do that more and more lately. Since my sixth birthday.

Pain seared my head as she wrapped her hand around my ponytail and jerked me to my feet. I couldn't let her hear me cry or this would get worse.

"Go!" she screamed in that voice that sent chills down my body. The hard shove from her hands sent me stumbling out of the closet and into the hallway. She would stay in the closet until I came back with the package.

I glanced back at her but instead of seeing her wild, distant eyes there was blood. It was pouring out of the room and into the hallway. No . . . no, there wasn't supposed to be blood.

Then a shrill scream of terror ripped from the small room.

◈

I jolted straight up and the scream was still echoing around me as it tore from my chest. It was my own scream. It was always my scream. Not my mother's.

I was still alone. Looking around the living room, I took slow, deep breaths while my heart kept hammering against my chest. I pulled my legs up and tucked my knees under my chest. Falling asleep without Woods here wasn't something I did often. Having him near me while I slept kept me from having night terrors for the most part.

The clock on the fridge said it was after nine. He should have been home over an hour ago. Had he stayed later with his mother? I reached for my phone on the coffee table and saw that I had two missed calls and one text message. All from Woods.

I clicked the text message.

Please answer. I'm worried about you and Mom passed
out during dinner. I think she hasn't been eating properly.
Call me!

That had been ten minutes ago. I jumped up from the
couch and started to dial his number when the front door
swung open and Woods came running inside. His eyes locked
on mine and he stopped and let out a deep breath. "Thank
God. Shit, baby, you scared me."

I dropped my phone and walked over to him. "I'm so sorry.
I just woke up. I fell asleep on the couch. How's your mother?"

Woods pulled me against him and wrapped his arms
around me. "She was too weak to stand up so I called an ambulance. Angelina kept saying it could be a stroke. She rode
in the ambulance with Mom so I could come back here and
check on you."

I pushed at his chest. "Go! Go to the hospital. No, wait, let
me get my shoes, I'm going, too."

"Are you sure? If you're tired I don't want to drag you to the
hospital. We could be there all night."

I slipped my feet into a pair of tennis shoes and ran my
hands through my hair. "I want to be with you."

Woods smiled and held out his hand for me. "Good. I
won't be able to focus if I'm worried about you here alone. If
you need to sleep, I can always hold you."

I tried not to think about the fact that Angelina was helping him take care of his mother. He had been able to leave her
knowing she would be there beside his mother. What was I good

for? He had to worry about me. I was weak and needy. I was one more thing for him to stress over. I wasn't any help at all.

"Stop frowning. She's gonna be okay. The paramedics said there's a good chance her potassium is low. They don't think it's a stroke but they said due to her heart rate we needed to admit her and let doctors check her out."

I nodded as he laced his fingers through mine. "Let's go," I told him.

I was going to find a way to be helpful. He needed someone to lean on right now and I was going to be that someone.

"Did you sleep okay without me here?" he asked as we stepped outside.

"Yes. I slept great," I lied, because telling him the truth would only have upset him.

Woods

Della had finally given in and curled up against me. She'd been asleep within minutes. It was after three in the morning and they had Mom in a room under observation. Angelina was in the room with her. It was better that way.

I wasn't stupid. I knew Angelina wasn't helping my mother out of the goodness of her heart. She had no goodness in her heart. She was doing it to get to me. It wasn't like my mother needed a live-in nurse. Just a friend, and Angelina was being her friend.

Della didn't seem to mind. I had been watching to make sure it didn't get to her. The moment it seemed like Della was upset about Angelina's still being in our lives in this capacity, I would end all connection with my mom until Angelina left. She would eventually leave anyway when she realized I didn't want her and nothing she did was going to change that. Della owned me. She always would.

Della started to whimper in her sleep. I pulled her into my lap, brushed her hair back off her face, and whispered in her ear. That always calmed her. She rarely had bad dreams anymore. I normally saw them coming on and stopped them before they could take over.

"I have you, I'm right here. You're in my arms and nothing can touch you, Della. Nothing, baby. I won't let it," I assured her as her breathing returned to normal and her body eased back into a peaceful sleep. Smiling, I pressed a kiss to the side of her hair. I liked knowing I could fight off her fear. It was a powerful drug to know all she needed was me.

"Doesn't that get exhausting? She's like a helpless, needy child." Angelina's icy voice annoyed me. I didn't look up at her. I'd rather have kept my focus on the woman in my arms.

"How's Mom?" I asked her.

"She's sleeping. She hasn't been eating well. I knew that but I can't force her to eat. I'm not a damn nurse. If you came to visit her more often she'd eat more. She misses you."

My mother had never missed me. She was my father's puppet. She wanted me around if he did. When she thought I was going to marry Angelina she wanted me around.

"You're choosing her over your mother and it's disappointing, Woods."

I lifted my eyes from Della's peaceful face. "No. My mother is choosing her wants over mine. I will not live my life the way she wants me to. I will love who the fuck I wanna love. She doesn't control that," I replied in a cold voice.

"You have the Kerrington Club to run, Woods. You need someone who can stand by you and help you. You have to take care of not only the club but her. She's a weight on you, not a help. You can't be a successful businessman with a burden like her," she said, pointing at Della.

I held her closer to my chest. I could do anything if I had Della. Anything.

"What you're not understanding—what my mother is not

understanding—is I can't live without Della. I can't breathe. I can't fucking concentrate. I need her. Just her. I can do anything if I have her with me. So take your snide comments and beliefs and leave me the hell alone. I know what I need and it will never be you. Did you hear that? Is it sinking in this time? It. Will. Never. Be. You."

Angelina opened her mouth and snapped it closed again. The bright red color on her face said I'd gotten through. She was furious. Good. About damn time. I didn't watch her leave. I dropped my gaze back down to Della. Just looking at her calmed me.

When the doctor came out four hours later to tell me that Mom was fine and wanted to see me, Della woke up and rubbed her eyes. I watched as the doctor looked her over appreciatively. I didn't like it when men looked at her like that but it was pointless to get mad. She was beautiful and sexy as hell. I just had to remind myself she was mine.

"Go on in and see her. I'm going to find some coffee," she said in a sleepy voice. "I'll get you some, too."

I pressed a kiss to her lips because I needed to taste her and I wanted the doctor to see exactly who she belonged to. She immediately responded by wrapping her arms around my neck and kissing me back.

"I love you," I said against her lips as I ended the kiss.

"I love you," she replied, then stood up.

She walked off in the short cut-off sweatpants she was wearing and one of my hoodies. She'd come with me in a tank top last night and gotten cold in the waiting room. I had gotten her a hoodie out of my truck.

"Is the woman in the room with your mom your sister?"

the doctor asked. I glanced over at him. He was too young to be a doctor, wasn't he?

"No," I replied, and walked past him toward my mother's room.

Angelina was sitting in the chair beside her bed looking at a magazine. She had stayed all night. Even after I'd said what I had. Either she was crazy or she really did like my mom.

"Hey, Mom," I said as I closed the door behind me.

"Hello," she replied. "Angelina said you stayed all night. You didn't have to do that."

I walked over and bent down and pressed a kiss to her forehead. "Yeah I did," I replied.

"Did you send the girl home?" The distaste in her voice wasn't missed.

"She went to get coffee," I replied. I wasn't going to fight with her over Della. "You need to eat more, Mom."

She sighed. "I know, but I just don't have an appetite anymore. I miss him."

He was an ass. He tried to control me and he lied to me. He also hurt Della and she knew about it. Forgiving those things was hard. The fact he'd hurt Della made it almost impossible. I couldn't say anything. I had nothing to say.

"I need to get to work. When they discharge you, call me and I'll come get you." Getting out of there was best. She was my mother and I loved her, but there was so much between us that needed to be forgiven. I couldn't stay there.

"I'll take her home. You go work. You're going to be exhausted since you didn't sleep all night." Angelina sounded so sincere. I didn't trust that.

"Okay, well, call if you need me," I said to my mother, and then turned and left the room.

Della stood outside the door holding two coffees. The concern in her eyes was the most sincere thing I'd seen that morning.

"Is she okay?" Della asked as she handed me a cup of bad hospital coffee.

"Yeah. She's fine. Let's go," I replied.

"Why don't I leave and you stay here? She's your mom." Della started to say more but I shook my head and stopped her.

"She's fine. She needs to eat more. I want to leave with you."

Della let out a weary sigh, then nodded her head. "Okay. If that's what you want."

Della

The bonfire lit up the dark beach. I stood watching everyone drink, dance, and laugh. Woods had left to deal with an issue with the staff. He was looking for someone to take over his old job but he hadn't found anyone yet. Right now he was doing everything himself and I could see he was growing weary.

I glanced over at the group of Woods's friends and I knew I was welcome. Bethy was laughing loudly and I was pretty sure she was drunk. But I needed time to think. I wasn't in the mood to pretend like my heart wasn't heavy. Woods had been on the phone with Angelina today when I'd walked into his office. They'd been talking about his mom and it had been friendly. She was taking a lot off him and I wanted to like her. To be thankful to her. I just couldn't.

Turning, I walked up to the parking lot. No one was up there partying and I could wait for Woods to get back. I needed to get in a better mood before he came back. The fact that I was a hindrance to him weighed heavily on me. It was getting worse every day.

If I could just get better . . . If I could just stop having bad dreams . . . If I could forget my past and move forward . . . If the

27

fear that I might go crazy wasn't haunting me every day . . . then I might be able to help him. I might be a support for him.

"Della." Angelina's voice surprised me. I turned to see her standing behind the building where the restrooms were located. The small amount of light the moon was supplying shone down on her.

"Yes," I replied, not sure if I should be worried about being alone with her or if I was just being silly.

"Where's Woods?" she asked.

"He had an issue with some of the staff. He's dealing with it."

Angelina looked disgusted. "He has so much on his shoulders and you make it so much worse. So helpless and fucked up. How long do you think he'll want you? What happens when that crazy in your genes takes over? He won't be able to keep you then. You'll be locked up. And I know he doesn't want kids with you. He would be worried about them being crazy, too. That would kill him."

Hearing my own fears spill from her cruel lips took my breath away. She was right. Everything she said was right. Woods and I pretended like the future was possible. But it wasn't. I would never be his future. I wasn't getting better.

"What do you want?" I asked.

"I want you to leave him alone. He deserves so much more," she spat.

He did. I agreed. "But that won't be you. You're not better," I replied, shooting an angry glare her way. Even if she couldn't see me in the darkness, I hoped she could feel my hatred for her.

She walked over toward me and I fought the urge to back away from her. I wasn't scared of her. I could hold my own.

"You're a crazy bitch. You know nothing. He loved it when

I sucked his dick. He'd scream my name and hold my head as if I had the key to heaven in my mouth. He loved it."

"Stop it!" I screamed. I didn't want to think about Woods and Angelina together. It made me ill.

"He once said my thighs were magical. He loved being between them."

"Shut up!" I said, backing away.

A pleased smirk touched her evil lips. "I can still make him hard. All I have to do is rub my hand over his crotch and talk dirty and he's hard as a rock."

I turned and started walking away before I threw up. My head jerked back and I cried out in pain as Angelina pulled my hair in her fisted hand. "You're not going anywhere, you crazy bitch." She growled and pulled me by my hair while I stumbled back into the darkness behind the building. Away from the parking lot where someone might see us.

"I swallowed his come. Do you do that for him? Do you go to his office just to suck his dick and make him cry out in pleasure? Does he tell you how amazing your mouth is? Hmm?"

Tears burned my eyes. The pain in my head was nothing compared to the pain from her words. I didn't want to think of Woods with her. It hurt too much.

She slung me down onto the grass and I glanced up to see a wild look in her eyes that scared me. What was wrong with her? Why were we back there in the dark? I scrambled to get up and she kicked me in the ribs, then pushed me back down on the ground. "He stays with you. Why? Why does he stay with you? I do everything for him! Everything! I am what he needs. I was raised to be his wife. I fit into his world. I can be his helpmate but he wants you! Why?!" she screamed, and reached for my hair again, only this time she pulled out a handful.

"If you're dead, then you won't be in my way. I can make it better for him. I can ease his pain. He'll be over you and fucking me against his desk again. Not you! *Me!*" She reached for my arm and then threw me on my back. I felt her pulling my hair again. I was going to black out. The darkness was going to take me and I would be lost in myself. She'd kill me then. If I didn't stay focused I wouldn't be able to fight her.

"I can strangle you. No one will ever know," she snarled. "You took him from me. You made him cheat on me. You're the reason he broke off our engagement. He was going to marry me. You made him leave me. Now I'm going to fix that."

I knew crazy. I had seen it all my life. And right now I was positive she wasn't kidding. This was no idle threat. Something had snapped in her head and she was going to kill me. I had to do something. With my side throbbing, I wasn't sure I could fight back. I would beg, then catch her off guard and knee her in the ribs.

"No, please. Just talk to Woods. I didn't do anything. I swear. Don't, oh God."

"I'm done talking to Woods. You took what was mine. He chose you. Fine. He can have your skanky, crazy ass. But first you're gonna fucking pay for taking what was mine." She slapped me across my face so hard everything went blurry. "Hurts, don't it, bitch? You're a psycho. Why Woods thinks you can make him happy, I don't know. He'll learn. He will fucking learn not to screw with me!" she roared, then kicked my sore ribs again, taking my breath away. I had to fight back. If she kept this up I wasn't going to be able to fight back.

I started to move when she grabbed my hair again and

jerked me up, only to slap me again. I couldn't keep from crying out in pain. I needed to focus on saving myself but the pain was overpowering me. My vision was blurring and I used all my willpower to push it away. I had to keep it from taking me away.

"Let her go." Blaire's voice came through the darkness like an avenging angel and I cried in relief. Then I turned to see her standing there with a gun pointed at Angelina. *Holy shit. She has a gun.*

"What the fuck?" Angelina said. Her hold on my hair only tightened. I should have done something to fight back now but I was more scared of the gun in Blaire's hands than of Angelina at the moment. Did she know how to use that thing?

"Let go of her hair and step away from her," Blaire said with command. I was impressed and terrified.

Angelina laughed. That was it. The girl was insane. She had a gun pointed at her and she was laughing. I was scared to breathe. "That's not even real. I'm not an idiot. Go mind your own fucking business and stop playing *Charlie's Angels*," Angelina said.

Blaire's gun made a sound that I knew meant she was ready to fire. I had heard that click on television before. "Listen, bitch. If I wanted to I could pierce both your ears from here and not mess your fucking hair up. Go ahead, test me." The look in Blaire's eyes might have been meant to warn Angelina but I could detect the truth in her words. I believed her and the relief washed over me. She could actually use that thing.

Angelina let go of me and I quickly moved away from her while I had a chance. I believed Blaire could use that gun but I didn't want to be anywhere near her target.

"Do you have any idea who I am? I could end you. Your ass is going to sit in jail for a very long time for this," Angelina said, but the fear in her voice wasn't lost on me, and I doubted Blaire missed it, too.

"We're in the dark and there are three of us. You don't have a scratch on you. Della's bleeding and bruised and it's our word against yours. I don't care who you are. This doesn't look good for you."

Angelina moved back as if she could run from a bullet. "My daddy will hear about this. He'll believe me," she said with a shaky voice.

"Good. My husband will hear about it, too, and he'll sure as hell believe me," Blaire replied.

Angelina laughed. "My daddy can buy this town. You have fucked with the wrong woman."

"Really? Bring it on, 'cause right now you're looking at a woman with a loaded gun who can hit a moving target. So please. Bring. It. On," Blaire replied like a complete badass. I wanted to be like her. I wanted to be tough.

I pulled my legs up and wrapped my arms around my knees and prayed this would end without her having to use that gun.

"Who are you?" Angelina asked. I hadn't realized that Angelina didn't know who Rush Finlay's wife was. He was a celebrity because of his father. I thought the whole world knew who Blaire was.

"Blaire Finlay," she replied.

"Shit. Rush Finlay married a hick with a gun. I find this hard to believe," Angelina said in her snide, uppity tone. She really did think she was above everyone else.

"I'd believe her. She's holding the fucking gun." Rush's voice came from behind Blaire. I let out the breath I was holding. *Thank God he's here.*

"Are you kidding me? This town is insane. All of you," Angelina said, on the verge of a scream.

"You were the one beating up an innocent woman over a man in the dark," Blaire replied. "You're the one who looks insane here."

"Fine. I'm over this. I'm done," Angelina yelled, and walked over to the parking lot. I sat in shock as Blaire lowered the gun and put the safety back on before handing it to Rush. She then ran over to me. I just sat there and stared up at her. She'd just pulled a gun on another woman for me. I couldn't wrap my head around everything that had happened. I felt the darkness around my eyes start to close in on me. I had to fight off the panic attack I knew was close.

"Did you really just pull a gun on her?" I asked, trying to focus on the here and now.

"She was putting a beating on you," Blaire said simply.

"Ohmigod. She's crazy. I swear, I was beginning to think she was going to beat me until I was unconscious. I kept thinking I was going to zone out and then she'd really hurt me." I looked up at her. "Thank you." Those two words weren't enough but it was all I could say right now. I was about to lose myself. The darkness was coming.

Blaire held out her hand. "Can you stand up? Or do you want to sit here while I call Woods?" I needed to stand up. I had to fight this. I slipped my hand into hers.

"I want to stand. I need to stand up," I told her. I didn't want to tell her I was about to black out. It was a weakness that I was ashamed of. Having her see me like that would be humiliating. Rush would know Woods was in love with a crazy woman. I couldn't do that to him.

Blaire pulled me up, then asked, "You got a phone?"

I couldn't talk. I needed to stay focused. I handed it to her.

She was calling Woods. I knew that. I wanted her to call him. If he held me I could fight this. Blaire handed me the phone. I would have to talk to him.

"Baby?" His voice came over the line and my fear eased off.

"Hey," I replied.

"You okay?" he asked. I could tell he was walking. Hopefully he was headed back this way.

"Actually, no, not really. I had an incident with Angelina," I explained.

"Did she say something to upset you? Is she still there? Put the bitch on the phone." I heard his truck crank up. He was already heading back.

"No . . . no . . . she's gone. Uh, Blaire showed up and . . . uh, scared her off," I tried to explain, though I wasn't sure how to.

"Scared her off? What the hell did she do to you? Are you alone?" The panic in his voice was nothing compared to what he was going to feel when he found out what really happened.

"Blaire is still here and so is her husband," I reassured him.

"Rush is there? Good. Stay with them. Where are you?"

"Behind the parking attendant building."

"I'm almost there. I love you, stay with me. Don't black out. I'm coming."

"Okay. I love you, too," I replied. He knew I was close to getting lost in the monsters in my mind.

I hung up and looked over at Blaire. "He's on his way."

"Good. We'll wait with you," she replied, then opened her purse and pulled out a wet wipe. "You want to clean the blood off your lip before he gets here and goes after Angelina?" she asked, holding it out to me.

I hadn't realized I was bleeding. I took it from her. "Thanks."

The sound of Woods's truck broke through the silence and I wanted to weep in relief. He was here. His door swung open and he jumped down and came running over to me. I felt like sagging in relief. He was here and I was okay.

"Dammit!" he roared, furious, as he took in my face. He pulled me into his arms and held me tightly. His breathing was fast and hard. He was upset. "God, baby, I am so sorry. She's gonna pay for this," he said as his hands starting roaming my body to make sure I was okay. I wasn't okay. But I would be.

"It's fine. I think Blaire scared her," I assured him.

"What did Blaire do?" he asked.

"She pointed a gun at her and threatened to pierce her ears," I explained.

Woods cocked an eyebrow. "So, Alabama pulled her gun out again? Thanks, Blaire," he said before kissing my head. "I love you. I'm here and you're going to be okay. Stay with me. I got you," he whispered in my ear. He knew I didn't want them to know how close I was to getting lost in my head.

"I'm glad I found them. You need to do something about that woman; she's a crazy bitch," Blaire said, then turned to walk back to Rush.

"Thank you," I called out after her. She'd literally saved my life.

"You're welcome," she replied with a sweet smile. She didn't look like someone who had just pointed a gun and threatened to pierce someone's ears with it. I now knew that under that beautiful, innocent-looking exterior, Blaire Finlay was a tough badass. I wanted to be her one day.

Woods

I turned on the shower, then reached for Della. Streaks of blood were still visible on her face. She'd tried to clean it but she'd left some of the proof behind. A bruise was forming on her face and blades of grass in her hair clung to the tangled mess.

She wouldn't let me call the police. She'd cried and begged me not to. I was going to kill Angelina myself. She'd hurt the most precious thing in my life and she would pay for it. I'd make sure she paid over and over again. But right now I had to keep Della lucid and out of her head.

I reached for her shirt and had started to lift it over her head when she cried out in pain. I froze. "What's wrong, baby?"

"My ribs," she said in a tight whisper.

Fuck. I forced myself to calm down. The anger rolling over me was getting worse. I was going to snap. The tank top she was wearing was ruined. Blood and grass stains had made it unsalvageable. I reached up and grabbed the neckline, then ripped it in one swift move. It fell to the ground behind her and my eyes found the bruised skin. It was too much. Seeing the dark bruise covering her side broke me. I had let this happen to her. I had left her alone and let this woman into our lives. This was my fault.

My knees gave out and I fell before her. Knowing that she

was hurting was too much. The sob that filled the bathroom was mine.

"Woods, please don't," her sweet voice begged. Della's hands caressed my head in her attempt to comfort me. Me. I wasn't the one who had been attacked. She was the one with bruises and covered in blood but I was the one on his knees, crying. "It's okay, I'm okay," she tried to reassure me. She was in pain and she was worrying over me. I was a man, dammit. I couldn't break apart on her. It was my place to take care of her, not the other way around.

I forced myself to stand up and focus on undressing her. I needed to clean her. I had to fix her. Make the pain go away.

"Woods?" Her voice was soft and unsure. I knew the tears were still rolling down my face silently. I couldn't seem to make them stop. I was trying. They weren't going away.

"I need to clean you. Let me clean you," I said, finally lifting my eyes to look into hers. She wasn't about to leave me anymore. The glazed look that I'd seen in her eyes earlier was gone. I had her back with me.

"Okay," she said simply, and stepped into the shower.

I undressed and followed her inside. She wasn't standing under the warm water.

"I need to wash your hair," I told her, moving close to her body and running my hands down her arms.

"Be gentle with my head," she said.

Her head? What the fuck did Angelina do to her head? "What's wrong with your head, baby?"

She dropped her eyes from mine as she stared down at the marble floor. "She pulled a lot of my hair out. It burns," she said so softly I almost missed it.

My body trembled. *Holy hell.*

"I will be gentle. But we need to clean it. Do you trust me?" I asked as she stared warily back at the water. Then she nodded.

I moved her under the water and pressed kisses to her lips while whispering comforting words to her as she winced.

Gently, I washed her hair, then moved to clean her body. She flinched as I touched the tender spots. Each flinch from her body caused my chest to constrict. Once she was clean I wrapped a towel around her and carried her to bed. I needed to hold her but first I wanted her checked out.

"I'm going to call a friend of mine. He'll come here and check you out. I need to know you're okay. Your ribs could be broken."

She started to shake her head but I couldn't give her this. I had to know she was okay. "Della, I have to. I can't not make sure you're okay. Please, baby. He's a sports doctor. We use him at the club during tennis tournaments. He's a friend. It's okay."

She finally nodded. "Okay," she agreed.

I didn't want to leave her in there alone but I wanted to talk to Martin without her hearing me. I didn't want to scare her.

"Hello," Martin said after one ring. I had his private line for emergencies. The club had been using him for over twenty years.

"Martin, it's Woods. I need you to make a house call. My girlfriend was beaten up tonight by my crazy ex-fiancée. I'm worried her ribs could be broken or she could be internally bleeding. I don't think Angelina is strong enough to actually cause internal bleeding but I still need Della checked out. She won't go to the hospital."

Martin let out a low whistle. "Damn, Woods. That is some fucked-up shit," he replied.

"Yeah, it is. Can you come check her tonight?"

"I'm on my way. I'll be there in twenty minutes. Are y'all at your house?"

"Yeah, thanks, man. See you in a few."

◇

Della hadn't been thrilled about Martin checking her out, but I'd held her hand while he felt her ribs. She was bruised but that was it. He'd left her some pain pills. They had successfully knocked Della out within thirty minutes. I wasn't going to be able to sleep, though. I had something I needed to do.

Jace arrived ten minutes after I called him. He didn't ask questions. He just agreed to watch Della and call me if she woke up. He seemed to understand that I wasn't ready to talk about this. I started for the door.

"Don't do anything that could take you away from her. Be careful how you handle this. Don't kill a bitch; I don't want your ass in jail. I would want revenge too. Just . . . just be careful. Use your head."

Rush must have told him. I didn't look back at him. I only nodded, then opened the door and headed outside. I was going to make sure Angelina understood that this was her only warning. She had one hour to get her shit and get on a plane and not come back. I couldn't beat the hell out of a woman but I could make her wish she'd never been born. She'd crossed a line.

When I drove up to my mother's house, Angelina's car was missing. She was hiding or she wasn't home yet. I took the stairs to my mother's house two at a time and knocked once before pulling out my key and opening the door.

My mother was walking down the staircase in her robe. "Woods? What are you doing here so late? You scared me."

"Where is she?" I asked, trying to control the anger in my voice.

"She left. What did you do?"

I let out a hard laugh. "What did I do? I just stood over Della as a doctor checked her for internal bleeding and broken ribs because Angelina beat the shit out of her. If Blaire Finlay hadn't shown up and pulled a gun on her crazy ass she would have killed Della. So tell me now, where is she!"

Mother covered her mouth with both her hands as her eyes went round in surprise. "What? That's . . . that's ridiculous. Angelina is a sweet girl. She'd never do something so awful. Della has lied to you."

"No, Mother. Rush and Blaire Finlay found them and stopped Angelina. I have witnesses. She isn't sweet, she was using you to stay near me. She's a fucking psycho."

"Watch your mouth in my house. I won't listen to this. The poor girl left here in tears saying you'd hurt her too many times. She wanted to stay with me but she was going home to her parents and starting over."

She was going to refuse to believe me. I shouldn't have been surprised. She had always chosen my father over me. Now she was choosing Angelina because she was my father's choice for me. What mattered was that Angelina was gone. The bitch was gone. She had better never come back.

"If you speak to her, let her know that if she steps foot in Rosemary again I will have her arrested. I have witnesses and I will press charges. I don't give a fuck who her daddy is."

I didn't wait for my mother to respond. I turned and left the house, slamming the door behind me.

Della

I stared down at my phone after I hung up with Woods. He had called me four times today already to check on me. It had been this way all week. Since Angelina had attacked me he had been afraid to leave me. He had a country club to run but he kept calling me. I mentioned getting a job again and he panicked and begged me not to. He said he couldn't focus on work if he was worrying about me.

We were at a standstill. This wasn't healthy. He needed to be able to live without worrying over me. I needed to be able to live. His protective nature was starting to smother me and I loved him too much to hurt him by saying something about it. I was going to have bad moments. I was going to slip into my head sometimes and he couldn't always be there for me. I just didn't know how to get him to understand this and accept it. How could we make this work? This couldn't be forever.

I wanted this forever but Woods deserved so much more. I was holding him back. This relationship would destroy him. I would destroy him. I felt sick to my stomach. *I did this. I let this happen. I let myself fall so helplessly in love with him. I let myself believe he could fix me. That we could fix me. But it isn't happening.*

My phone rang and I looked down to see Tripp's number.

He hadn't called in two weeks. I thought about telling Woods that Tripp checked in with me a couple times a month, but I hadn't found the right words to explain that. Woods seemed jealous of Tripp. He had no reason to be, but he was. I didn't want to give him something else to worry over.

"Hello," I said as I stretched my legs in front of me on the sandy beach.

"How are things?"

"Good, I guess," I replied.

"You guess? That don't sound good."

"Angelina beat me up and Blaire Finlay pulled a gun on her and scared her off. Woods is now more overprotective than ever and he's always worried about me."

Tripp was quiet for a moment. I let him digest my words.

"Holy shit. Blaire has a gun?"

I laughed. *That* was his response to what I'd just told him?

"Sorry. I don't think that was the point. But damn, I can't picture that hot little blonde with a gun."

"Yeah, it was a shock," I replied, smiling out at the water crashing against the shore.

"Jace said she was from Alabama. Maybe I've been looking for a woman in the wrong states. I need to try out good ole Alabama next."

Tripp always managed to make me laugh, and he made me forget for a moment that my chest was about to explode from pain.

"Thanks," I said.

"For what?"

"Making me laugh," I replied.

"Anytime."

We sat there again for a few moments in silence.

"Where are you at now?" I asked, knowing he was on a road trip.

"I'm in South Carolina at a place called Myrtle Beach. I like it here."

"You like those beaches, don't you?" I replied.

"Makes me feel like I'm home, in a way."

"Will you ever come back here to stay?"

He didn't respond right away. It made me wonder what kept him away. There were secrets that he wouldn't share with me.

"Doubt it," he finally said.

"I don't think I can stay," I said aloud for the first time.

"Why?"

"Because this isn't working. I'm holding him back. I'm not getting better. This isn't going away and he deserves more. He needs more. Someone strong to stand beside him."

"He wants you, Della."

"Sometimes what we want isn't what's best for us," I replied.

"Yeah . . . I know that," he said quietly. "But if you leave him it will break him."

It would shatter me. But I loved him too much to ruin his future. "He will heal and then the woman who can be all he needs will walk into his life one day and he'll be glad he didn't make the mistake of staying with me."

"Don't say that. You aren't a mistake. You underestimate your worth. You make him happy. Woods is happy with you."

"For now he is," I replied.

Tripp sighed. I was frustrating him, but he knew deep

down that I was right. "When the time comes and you think you need to leave, just call me. Don't go by yourself."

"Okay," I replied. I would call him when I needed to. He wasn't tied to me. I didn't control his actions and thoughts. I could travel with Tripp and not destroy his future. At least until I was stable enough to live alone.

"I think you need to talk to Woods about this first. Don't blindside him."

I wasn't sure that was possible. He would never listen to me. "Okay," I replied.

◇

I stepped out of my car and waved at Bethy as she drove by in a golf cart toward the fifteenth hole. She was a cart girl at the Kerrington Club. It was how she had met Jace. He was a member here and I had heard them arguing over her quitting more than once. He hated seeing the men on the course flirt with her. That had been him once. She refused to change just because she was dating him. I think, deep down, he respected her for that.

After hanging up the phone with Tripp, I'd sat and thought a long time. Woods needed help and all I seemed to be doing was whining over not having a job and being a burden on him. I was stronger than that. Why couldn't I help him? I could. He would have me close by and I would have a purpose. So, I'd gone back to the house and dressed up.

I was going to go apply for a job as his assistant. I could do the tasks that caused him extra headaches. I could handle the staff. I might have been dealing with some mental issues, but I wasn't helpless. If I could prove to myself that I could do this, then I could prove to Woods and the rest of the world that I was healing.

Vince glanced up at me and smiled. "Go on in, Miss Sloane," he said before going back to his work. Woods had informed him that I never needed permission to enter. I was free to come and go as I wanted.

I knocked, then opened the door.

"I realize that, but make it happen. I need the order here tomorrow, not Monday. I'll switch suppliers if it doesn't happen," Woods said.

"Yes, sir, Mr. Kerrington, we will make it work," the voice said from his speakerphone.

"Good," he replied, then ended the call before standing up and walking toward me.

"I needed to see you," he said, smiling as he pulled me into his arms. I put both my hands up to stop him before he could kiss me. If I let him kiss me I would end up forgetting my purpose here, and there was a good chance that we would be naked in minutes.

"I'm here to apply for a position as your assistant," I said.

That stopped him. He gazed down at me, confused, and I used the opportunity to sell my idea. "You need someone to handle the staff and place orders. You have bigger things to deal with. I can handle the staff. I can put out the small fires and leave the big ones to you. I can place orders and I can help you. I can't sit home alone and lost. I can be here near you and helping you every day." I stopped and took a breath. He hadn't moved, but I had his complete attention.

Finally, he stepped back enough so that he could see the pencil skirt and pair of heels I'd put on. I was even wearing a nice blouse and had pulled my hair up in a bun with chop-sticks pushed through it. It was as professional as I could get with what I had to work with. A small smile tugged on his lips.

"Is this your interview outfit?" he asked.

I nodded and continued to watch him.

"You want to be my assistant. To help me. Looking like that," he said.

Again, I just nodded. Then he chuckled and shook his head. "Baby, I don't doubt that you would be able to help me, but if you intend to strut around here dressed like that, I'm going to end up fucking you every damn hour, or thinking about fucking you every damn minute."

My stomach fluttered hearing him say he was going to fuck me. I had to stay focused. "I can wear something else," I replied.

Woods studied me a moment. "You sure you want to do this?"

He wasn't going to tell me no. I tamped down my excitement. "Yes. Please. I want to do something. You know I want a job, but more than that I want to help you."

"Are you going to file a sexual harassment suit against me when I decide what I need is to touch you?"

I shook my head and grinned this time. "No. But that's not what I'm here for. I want to take some stress off you," I told him.

"Oh, that would take stress off me," he said, putting his hand on my hip and pulling me against him. "You're hired. But the minute you feel like it's too much, you tell me."

I squealed and reached up to grab his head and kiss him hard on the mouth. "Thank you, boss. I swear I'll do a good job. You just have to swear to give me stuff to do. I want to take stuff off your plate."

"You can take off my clothes," he said against my mouth before tracing kisses down my neck. I arched into him. His tongue flicked over my skin, causing me to shiver. "You can start working for me after I've had you in this sexy little outfit. Then you need to change. Because I won't be able to concentrate with you dressed like this. All I can think about is the way I want to be buried deep inside my new assistant."

His hand slid up my skirt and slipped inside the crotch of my panties. "All wet," he replied before sliding his finger inside me.

"Oh," I cried out, and his mouth got hungrier.

"Unbutton this shirt," he growled.

I did as he asked and his mouth worshipped the tops of my breasts as his finger continued to fuck me. "On my desk," he said, picking me up and putting me on his desk, then shoving my skirt up.

I watched him pull my panties down. Then he fell to his knees and spread my legs, putting my feet up on the edge of his desk. "Fuck, you smell good," he swore before his tongue began tracing circles around my clit, then dipping inside of me. All I could do was squirm and beg. He kept up the torture until I was chanting, "Please, Woods, please."

Finally, his tongue flicked over my clit, sending me rocketing toward my release. Before I could see clearly again, Woods was over me and stretching me as he entered me. I loved it when he filled me up.

"Heaven. This is my heaven. All I fucking need to breathe," he said as he shifted his hips, moving in and out of me.

I pushed papers out of the way and leaned back on my arms to brace myself. Woods's shirt was still on and I wished it wasn't. I loved seeing the muscles in his arms flex when he hovered over me. "You didn't unbutton your shirt," I said as a moan of pleasure escaped me.

He smirked. "You wanted my shirt off?"

I nodded and lifted my legs to wrap them around his waist.

"Next time, baby. I can't stop now," he growled.

I slid my legs up his back higher and he groaned, then threw his head back. I felt him grow inside me and I came apart underneath him as his hot seed poured into me.

I fell back on my elbows and gasped for air.

Woods's head dropped onto my chest and he took several deep breaths.

"Best interview ever," he panted out.

I let out a giggle that only caused him to laugh against my skin. I was going to make myself worthy of this man.

Woods

I stood just out of sight as Della calmed the feuding cooks. I wanted to handle this. I hated having to watch her stand between two men yelling at each other. But I couldn't interfere. She was so happy with her new job. At first I hadn't wanted to give her much work, but she'd put her hands on her hips and pitched a fit one day when she saw me outside dealing with a staff issue. Once I realized this was going to make her happy, I let her have more of my work.

She was good at it, too. Not once all week had she had an episode. I had been watching her closely, and I had others watching her to make sure she didn't need me. I was getting more done knowing I could just check on her at any minute. And she was in my office a lot. We were having a hell of a lot of office sex, too, which was making me very happy. Vince wasn't thrilled about it but he didn't complain too much.

"How're things working out with your new assistant?" Jace asked in an amused tone. I turned to see him dressed to play golf.

"She's very good at what she does," I replied.

Jace chuckled and looked over my shoulder as she calmed down the cooks. They were both looking at her now. She was hard not to look at when she was all fired up and red in the face. If the new waiter didn't stop looking at her like he wanted a bite, I was gonna have to fire his ass.

"Want to grab some lunch? I was gonna eat before my tee time."

I was going to ask Della to eat lunch with me but she had several things to do and I knew she'd turn me down so she could work instead. I nodded. "Yeah, sounds good."

We walked around to the entrance and the hostess smiled up at us as we went toward my table. Della came into the dining room and spoke with the hostess, then headed over to Jimmy. She had been a server when she'd first come here and Jimmy had become one of her friends. I was good with that since I knew Jimmy had more interest in me than her.

"She looks so professional," Jace drawled.

I knew he was looking at her skirt and heels and that damn bun in her hair. It was driving me nuts. She said she needed to dress this way to appear professional, but I'll be damned if she didn't look like a fantasy.

"Don't look at her," I snarled.

Jace chuckled. "Relax, man. Not interested in your woman. I have my own."

I knew this but I was feeling territorial watching her move around dressed like that and drawing attention to herself. She was writing something down on a small notepad. Jimmy was probably telling her the things the servers needed ordered. He was the head server. She put the tip of the pen she was writing with in her mouth and chewed on it as she listened to Jimmy, then went back to writing.

"Heard anything from the crazy bitch?" Jace asked.

Angelina had disappeared and I liked it that way. I had to check on my mother more and that was a pain in the ass because she was mad at me. She still believed that Angelina was innocent and I was the asshole who had run her off.

"No, and if she knows what's good for her she won't ever come near me or Della again."

The new server who had been looking at Della in ways he shouldn't have walked over to her and said something that made her smile. She nodded her head and then glanced over his shoulder to see me watching her. The smile on her lips grew before she shifted her eyes back to the guy. I saw her say something to him before turning back to Jimmy, who had an annoyed expression on his face. That told me enough.

Jimmy nodded his head my way and said something to the guy, who glanced back at my table, then walked over to us. Jimmy had sent him to wait on us. Good man.

"Hello, Mr. Kerrington, what can I get you to drink?" the server asked as he filled our water glasses.

"Della is mine. Keep your distance. If you need something, ask Jimmy. He tells Della what is needed. Not you," I told him without caring that my tone was more angry boyfriend than boss.

His eyes went wide and he nodded. "Yes, sir," he replied.

"Get me a sweet tea," Jace said.

"Coffee," I told him, and then turned my attention back to Della, who was standing back, waiting to approach me. She looked wary.

"Hey, baby," I replied, standing up and walking over to her. She smiled at me, then glanced back at the server, who had just walked away.

"What did you say to Ken?" she asked.

"He doesn't need to be looking at you and talking to you. He needs to be working," I told her.

She pressed her lips together, then nodded. "Okay. But he's new. You just hired him last week."

I slipped my arm around her. "Yes he is, and I understand that. He should have been worried about the fact that his boss had just been seated and needed to be waited on. Not the incredibly hot female talking to Jimmy."

Della shook her head, then laughed. "Okay, fine. But be nice. Jimmy needs help."

"Eat with us," I told her.

"Can't. I have to place an order for new aprons and there's an issue with the hot-tea button on the machine. I have to get the service guy here to fix it."

"You have to eat," I told her.

"I'm eating a late lunch with Blaire," she informed me, then grinned. "Now, let me work, boss."

I lowered my head to her ear. "Call me *boss* again and we're gonna end up in a cleaning closet real damn fast."

Della shoved away from me, laughing as she walked off.

I loved that girl.

Della

Blaire had called and asked me to have lunch with her that day. I hadn't spoken to her since the incident with Angelina except for the few times I'd seen her with Rush around the club. It was odd because I felt like we had a bond now that we'd faced down Angelina together. She'd been my hero that night. She made me want to be tough. I wasn't tough and I wanted to be so bad.

I walked out of Woods's old office, which he'd moved me into and told me to decorate any way I wanted. Blaire was headed toward me.

"You even have an office now," Blaire said, smiling brightly. I had to admit I loved having an office. Specifically this office. I had many good memories there. I didn't intend to change anything about it.

"Yes, I feel very official," I replied.

"Good. I'm glad Woods has you. You're perfect for him."

I didn't agree with her. He could have done better—so much better—but I was working toward being good enough. Strong enough. Tough enough.

"Ready for lunch?" I asked, wanting to change the subject.

"I'm starving. Nate isn't sleeping as much as he used to. He keeps me busy but it's wonderful. Downside is, I don't have a lot of time to eat. When Rush is home he helps out a ton and makes sure I have time to eat. Anyway, I'm ready for a baby-free meal."

Nate was Rush and Blaire's baby boy. He was an adorable mixture of the two of them. I didn't normally think guys with piercings and that rough rock star look were attractive, but Rush Finlay holding a baby in his arms was very nice to look at.

"Is Rush with Nate now?" I asked as we walked to the dining room.

"Yes. They're going fishing, which means Nate is going to sit on a blanket and eat sand, if he can get to the edge of the blanket, and Rush is going to fish for about five minutes before realizing he can't fish and watch Nate at the same time. Then he'll stop fishing and they'll sit at the edge of the water and let their feet get wet."

The happiness in Blaire's voice was unmistakable. Rush Finlay made her happy. She made him happy. That was what I had with Woods but it was different. Rush could leave her alone with their baby and not worry about her zoning out and getting lost in her head. He could love her and not worry that his baby would inherit her mental illness. Their love was easy. It was the kind that would go the distance. What Woods and I had wasn't.

Every time I saw Rush holding his baby, I wanted that for Woods. The proud look in his eyes and joy on his face. I couldn't give him that.

"You okay?" Blaire's voice broke into my thoughts and I forced a smile.

"I'm sorry. Work on the brain. I promise to shut it off and be a good lunch date," I assured her.

"As long as it's work that's causing that distressed look on your face," Blaire replied, sounding like she didn't believe me.

I hadn't been brave enough to talk to my best friend, Braden, about this. She loved me fiercely and thought I could do no wrong. She also thought I could be a mother and stable wife. She lived in a fairy tale that I didn't allow myself to step into. Would Blaire be the same way, or would she see my side and understand my fears?

The hostess snapped to attention when she saw me and led us to Woods's table. He had told the staff in the dining room that his table should be available at my convenience.

"Oh, we get the good table," Blaire said, grinning, as we sat down. "I guess you're the boss now, too."

"Woods made a big deal out of them always seating me here." I felt myself blush and Blaire laughed.

"That's sweet," she said.

I wasn't sure how to respond to that. It was sweet. Woods was always sweet. He was impossible to get mad at. Even when he deserved it. Like when he made the new server, Ken, almost pee his pants for talking to me.

Jimmy came strutting out of the kitchen, grinning at us.

"Looks like we're going to get special service, too," I said, nodding my head toward Jimmy.

"Well, hello, my beauties. I didn't know I was gonna get this lucky today," he said with a southern drawl that made most women drool over him.

"Hello, Jimmy," Blaire said.

"You broke loose from baby duty, I see," he teased.

"It's never a duty," she replied.

"Sweet tea for both of you?" he asked.

"Sparkling mineral water for me," Blaire told him.

His eyebrows shot up and then he laughed. "Well look at Alabama getting all sophisticated with her water choices. Damn, baby girl, I remember when you drank water out of the tap."

Blaire laughed. "It's better for the baby than soda or tea. That's all."

"Mmm-hmm, next you're gonna be ordering sushi with that raw shit in it," he said, shaking his finger at her. Then he shot us both a wink and turned to head back to the kitchen.

"He's a mess," Blaire said with fondness in her tone.

"Yes he is, but he runs the kitchen so well. I don't know what we'd do without him."

Blaire leaned back in her seat and crossed her legs. "You'd beg and plead with him to come back. That's what you'd do."

She knew exactly how important he was. She had once been a server there, too. Jimmy had been her first friend in Rosemary. The story went that she came into town looking for her daddy and found her daddy's new wife's son instead. Rush Finlay wasn't a fan of her father and disliked her on the spot. But he let her live in the maid's room while she worked for Woods and made some money until her dad got back from France with Rush's mom.

Rush treated her poorly but ended up falling for her against his will. They had more pain to work through in the end and a lie that tore them apart. I wouldn't have believed any of it seeing them now, but Bethy had told me all about it. She'd been Blaire's friend through it all.

"Did my gun effectively run off the wicked witch, or did Woods do that?" Blaire asked.

"I think it was your gun and the fact that she was scared of what Woods would do once he found out. She left that night and we haven't seen or heard from her since. Mrs. Kerrington isn't very happy with Woods about the whole thing. She blames him for her leaving."

"You're welcome to tell her that it was all me," Blaire said with a smile.

"Thank you, but I don't think it will matter. She doesn't approve of me. She wants Angelina for Woods."

Blaire sighed. "I understand that. I have a mother-in-law who hates me so badly she hasn't even seen her only grandchild."

Blaire was poised and beautiful. She wasn't dealing with something like a mental illness, so you would think her mother-in-law would have loved her. But she represented something to Rush's mother that couldn't ever go away. It was part of the dark past she shared with Blaire's dad.

"I heard Rush's dad was in town last week visiting Nate," I said, remembering how the entire club had talked nonstop about the drummer from Slacker Demon being in town. He was a legend, just like the rock band he was a part of.

"Yes. Dean is a wonderful grandfather. It is a bit surreal to see him cuddling with Nate and singing to him. Nate adores the man. I love to watch Rush's face while he witnesses his dad with his son. It brings me to tears every time."

"I would imagine that is special," I replied. I didn't have parents who would see any child I might have one day. If I ever felt safe enough to have a child.

Woods

My mother was driving me nuts. She was lonely. I understood that. With Angelina gone, she spent most of her time alone. Mother had never done well alone. I had seen her at the club playing tennis with a few of her friends earlier in the week. She had put on a good show for them, treating me like she was proud of me. But I knew she was still mad at me. I'd been going along with her acting all my life.

I had sent Della to my office to organize some files on my desk that didn't really need organizing. I just wanted her safely out of the way while Mother was here. I wasn't sure my mom could act as if she liked Della. And I wasn't going to have Della hurt or embarrassed.

The rest of the staff loved Della. When they saw her coming, everyone became happier and nicer. They didn't want to let her down. Whatever had been wrong the moment before they were willing to fix. It was helping me out a shit-ton. My jealousy over the fact that the males on my staff bent over backward to make her smile was difficult. But then who wouldn't want to make Della happy? I couldn't be mad at them for that. As long as they kept their hands off of her.

"Where's Della?" Marco, our golf pro, asked as he walked into the clubhouse.

"Why do you need Della?" I asked, reminding myself that this man was happily married.

"She was working on getting me a sub for next week. They're inducing Jill on Monday and I want to be with her and the baby the first week."

"I have her working on something. I'll check to make sure she has a sub for you. You should be with your wife and child," I replied.

"Thanks, Mr. Kerrington," he replied, and nodded before heading over to grab a water from the cooler.

The back door swung open and Vince stood there, looking wide-eyed. "Mr. Kerrington, sir, you need to come quick."

It was Della. I knew that look. She was having one of her episodes. *Shit!*

I ran for the door. "Where is she?" I asked him.

"In your office, sir. She came up to see you and then your mom stopped by. I tried to call you but it went to voice mail. Your mom went into the office to talk to Della. After she came out I heard Della whimpering. I knocked, sir, but she didn't respond so I went in."

"That's enough. I know the rest. Don't tell anyone about this, do you understand?" I waited until he nodded before I sprinted across the parking lot into the main offices. *My mother is off her damn leash. Fuck! I shouldn't have left Della alone for so long.*

Several people called my name as I ran for the stairs, not wanting to wait on the damn elevator. Taking the stairs two at a time, I reached the third floor in less than a minute. My office door was closed and I was thankful Vince hadn't left her exposed to whoever walked up there.

I swung the door open and scanned the room until I found her sitting against the wall with her knees pulled up to her chin. Her arms were wrapped around her legs and she was rocking back and forth, whimpering. I hated seeing her like this. She'd been doing so well. Her night terrors had eased off; she hadn't experienced any in a month, at least.

"Della." I called her name as I walked over to her, hoping she could hear me and my voice would draw her out. I bent down beside her and pulled her into my arms. She was stiff and cold.

"No, no, no, no, no," she chanted over and over.

"I have you, sweetheart. You're in my arms. I have you, Della. Shh, it's okay. Come back to me, baby. Please come back to me. I'm right here and I have you." I whispered in her ear how much I loved her; I wasn't going to let her go until her body started to ease.

Slowly, her arms loosened their grip around her legs and wrapped around me, and then she buried her face in my neck. She was back. I continued to tell her she was wonderful and she was mine and I would take care of her. Reassuring her reassured me that I had her. That she was here and I could take care of her. I had let her take on too much responsibility because she was good at it. I had started letting her work longer and I was checking on her less. This was my fault. My mother would never have gotten to her if I had been watching her closer.

"I'm sorry," Della said in a teary voice against my chest.

"Don't say that," I replied as I ran my hand over her hair

and down her back. "Please, baby, don't say that. I hate for you to think you have to say that."

She sniffled. "I need to be stronger. I want to be stronger. I want to be tough."

Did she not realize how fucking tough she was? She had lived a horror story for sixteen years of her life that had ended even more horrifically. And she still laughed and found reasons to smile. She was brave enough to live life, even after enduring the monsters that had terrorized her in her room as a child. And they weren't pretend. She'd faced real monsters and she had survived. There was no one as fucking tough as this woman.

"Della, you are tougher than anyone I know. Just because you have to protect yourself sometimes and fade away from me doesn't make you weak. You're a survivor. You are my inspiration and I love you. No matter what, I love you."

Della clung tighter to me. My mother had upset her. I would deal with her. She wouldn't get close to Della again, even if I had to ban her from the club. This would stop. I was done with my family hurting what was mine.

We sat there in silence. Della let me hold her as close as I needed to. She let me kiss her head and hands and run my hands over her arms and back to reassure myself she was okay.

The knock on the door ended our peace and quiet. Della started to move out of my lap but I held her to me. I was going to ignore whoever it was. Vince should have been out there by now.

"Is everything okay, sir?" Vince asked from the other side of the door.

"Yes, we're fine," I replied.

Della tilted her head back to look up at me. "Did he see me?"

I nodded. I didn't want to lie to her, even though I knew she hated for people to see her when she was like that.

"He's going to think I'm insane," she said with a defeated sigh.

I grabbed her chin and made her look up at me. "No, he won't. You aren't insane. You are intelligent, lovable, and beautiful. But you are *not* insane. You lived through hell and you beat it, Della. Most people can't overcome something like what you've overcome. Don't ever think you're less than amazing."

A small smile tugged at the corners of her lips. "You just love me," she said.

"More than life," I replied before pressing my lips to hers.

Della

Woods hadn't left me alone since my blackout yesterday. I knew he had work to do. I also had work to do, but he was keeping me by his side at home. Every time I mentioned going into the office, he did something to distract me. Oral sex on the kitchen counter had been his first tactic, and it worked. I had forgotten about anything but the way he made me feel.

Then he'd caught me sneaking off to take a shower when he was on a work-related phone call. I mentioned that we needed to get ready, and then he'd taken me against the shower wall. After he cut the water off and carried me to bed, we'd made love again.

Now he was outside on the phone again. I knew he was dealing with work from home and it only proved my point that I was hindering him. My weakness was a weight on him, but I wanted to help him. When he opened the door and stepped inside, I started to tell him that we should really go to work. I was going to fight off any sexual advances he tried to use to keep me there.

"That was Vince. I have two board members in my office that my mother contacted about some things she knows nothing about. I need to go into work to deal with them. I should be back in two hours max," he said before the door closed behind him.

He wasn't going to let me go. "I could go to work, too. There are things I didn't get done yesterday."

"No. I've got to concentrate on this meeting, and knowing you're there will distract me. I'll be worried about you. Just stay here and I promise I'll come right back."

He pressed a kiss to my lips before walking to the bedroom to get dressed. I stood there and let his words sink in. He was taking my job away. He was going to keep me here again. He was afraid of my being at work and having one of my episodes.

I had been working so hard to be tough. To ease his worries. One bad day and he had me in a glass box again. This wasn't fair. I wanted to live. I loved being close to him and having a purpose, knowing I was helping him. Staying here all the time was lonely. I couldn't do this again.

He walked out of the bedroom dressed in a suit and smiled at me. "We'll eat at that Italian place you love in Seaside tonight," he told me, as if that made this all okay.

Instead of telling him how I felt, I just nodded and kissed him back, then watched him leave. I didn't fight back. I just let him decide what I was going to do. This wasn't tough. Blaire wouldn't have let Rush do this. She would have fought back. She would have turned Alabama badass on him and gotten her way.

I had to show Woods that I could do this. I'd had one slipup but I was bigger than that. I could keep working. He needed me there. I was helping him. I was good at it.

I went to the bedroom and got ready for work.

◇

Facing Woods while he was in a meeting wasn't a wise decision. Instead, I finished the work I hadn't completed yesterday. I managed to schedule a stand-in golf pro, ordered new golf carts to replace two of our older ones, and met with the manager of the golf course, Darla, about using new vendors for snacks and adding some new beers.

It was three hours before I had a chance to meet with Woods. He hadn't called me yet so he wasn't even aware that he had gone over his two hours. Either he was still in a meeting or he was so swamped with work he had lost track of time.

Vince smiled at me with relief in his face when I walked off the elevator. "Miss Della, I'm so glad you're back today. You've been missed."

I needed to go ahead and deal with this thing with Vince. "Thank you," I said, stopping at his desk. "About yesterday, Vince, I'm sorry you saw me like that. I'm very thankful you went and got Woods for me. I have those episodes sometimes and I work hard to control them, but I didn't do a good job yesterday."

He held up his hand to stop me. "I don't need an explanation. If you need me I'm here. Don't you concern yourself with what I saw. That's between us and only us."

Tears stung my eyes and I only managed to nod. I glanced at the closed door to Woods's office. "Is he in there?"

Vince shook his head. "No, he left about fifteen minutes ago. He said he'd be back in thirty minutes for a conference call he's expecting."

Crap. Was I going to miss him? "Okay, thanks, Vince."

I went back to the elevator and changed my mind. I'd take the stairs. Woods normally took the stairs. I might miss him if I took the elevator.

The moment the door to the stairs closed behind me, I heard Woods's voice from below. Stopping, I considered going back into the office. I didn't want to eavesdrop.

"I don't know how you've dealt with the crazy as long as you have." Jace's voice stopped me from leaving, as did his words. I froze with my hand on the door.

"It was what I had to do. I couldn't just let her be alone. But it's affecting my work. At least when Angelina was here she helped." Woods's words were like cold water being poured over my head.

"You need to keep your ass away from her insane shit. You have a corporation to run. Dropping what you need to do to deal with one of her batshit crazy episodes isn't fair. You need to fix this problem." Jace's words made the numbness in my heart start to spread.

"I can't. How the hell do I do that?" Woods said in a frustrated growl.

I'd heard enough. I had to get away. I had to leave. I couldn't breathe. The darkness was closing in again, and this time I wasn't going to be here for everyone to witness it.

I forced a smile at Vince when I walked back out of the stairwell and headed for the elevator. He didn't ask and I didn't explain. I just kept my focus on the elevator doors. They opened and I stepped inside. Taking deep breaths, I fought off the darkness. I would not do this here. My craziness was affecting his work. *No, no!* I would stay focused.

When the doors opened, I stepped out and walked straight

to the parking lot. When I reached my car I got inside and reached for my phone.

"Tripp," I said when he answered.

"Yeah?"

"I need you to come get me. It's time I left," I replied.

He was silent.

"Trust me. I will tell you after you get here. Don't tell Woods. Just come get me. It's past time I left."

"What did he do?"

I let out a heavy sigh and grasped at the strength I hoped was inside me. "He wants out. My issues are too much for him. He just doesn't know how to tell me. Please, it's time I left. I want to live my life now."

"I'll be there by lunch tomorrow. I just have my bike."

"I'll pack light," I replied.

"You can ship everything else. I'll text you an address."

"Okay."

"You're sure about this?"

"Yes," I replied.

Woods

My mother had called two of the board members my dad was closest to and told them that I was letting Della work at the club. Then she'd proceeded to tell them Della was mentally unstable and dangerous. She'd gone as far as to make up shit about Della trying to hurt her. My mother had lost her mind.

Jace walked into my office after I'd had a long meeting with the two men and lost my argument about Della. They wanted background checks on her. I knew what they would find and I refused to do it. She wouldn't want that.

"You look ready to murder an entire village with your bare hands, bro. What's up?" I stormed past him and to the stairwell. I needed to yell and hit a wall. That was the safest place to do it.

I ran up two flights of stairs before I stopped and slammed my fist into the wall, cursing everyone responsible. Della didn't need this right now. She was doing so much better. How was I supposed to tell her about this?

"What happened?" Jace asked from behind me. I hadn't realized he had followed me.

"My fucking mother happened. Her and Angelina. They're evil and twisted. How is it that my mother is so damn screwed up? What happened to her and my father to make them such fucked-up individuals? To make them think they can control lives? They can't! This club is mine and if I want to fire every motherfucker on the board that my father set in place, I will! It's time for a new board anyway," I snarled, taking deep breaths to calm myself down.

"I don't know how you've dealt with the crazy as long as you have," Jace said, sitting down on the steps and watching me pace.

"It was what I had to do. I couldn't just let her be alone. But it's affecting my work. At least when Angelina was here she helped," I said.

"You need to keep your ass away from her insane shit. You have a corporation to run. Dropping what you need to do to deal with one of her batshit crazy episodes isn't fair. You need to fix this problem," Jace said, as if it were easy. How was I supposed to just turn away from my mother? I was all she had.

"I can't. How the hell do I do that?" I asked, stopping my pacing and leaning against the wall. If it was a choice between Della and my mother, I would choose Della. If she forced my hand, I was going to have to turn away from her. First, I needed to decide about the board. I needed a lawyer. My own lawyer, not my father's. I was done using the people he had set in place. Things were different now and I didn't need a crazy-ass phone call from my mother sending board members to my office questioning my decisions.

It was time I made sure this place was run by me. My board would be made up of people I trusted and confided in. It was time for a new generation.

"Jace," I said, turning to look at him.

"Yeah?"

"You ready to be a board member?"

Jace frowned. "What?"

"I'm getting a lawyer. I'm firing the old board and starting my own."

A grin spread across Jace's face. "Hell yeah," he replied.

For the first time since I'd gotten the call earlier that day, I felt lighter. I wasn't going to let my mother control me. I was in control. My grandfather had left it all to me. Even her home was now mine. If she wanted to fuck with my life I'd fuck with hers enough to make her stop. She was my mom, but Della was my life.

⬦

Four hours had passed since I'd left Della. Dammit. I'd lost track of time. Grabbing my phone, I headed out the door to my truck. My call went straight to her voice mail. Shit!

Della's car was in the driveway. She was there. Maybe she'd been outside when I'd called her. I had promised her dinner tonight in Seaside. I was two hours late. This wasn't fair to her. I couldn't keep her here all the time. She was coming back to work with me. I needed her help. She was good at her job.

Opening the door, the smell of roasted garlic and tomatoes met my nose. I closed it and followed the smell to the kitchen. Della was standing at the stove with a black apron on from the club, stirring a pot.

"Hey," I said quietly so I didn't startle her.

She spun around and smiled at me. There was a sadness in her eyes she couldn't hide. I'd made her sad. My leaving her here had upset her. She had wanted to go to work today. I would have to explain all that tonight.

"I decided to cook instead of us going out," she said.

I walked over to stand behind her and wrapped my hands around her waist. "It smells incredible."

"Good. I haven't made lasagna in a long time. This sauce is hard to get right."

Something was off in her voice. I hated that she was upset.

"I'm sorry about today."

"Don't apologize. Please, don't. You had work to do. I know that and I'm okay with it."

She didn't want my apology. What was upsetting her then?

"You can come back to work tomorrow," I told her.

"I don't think I'm ready for that yet," she replied.

She wasn't ready for it? Today she'd tried several times to go back to work. What had changed?

"Why do you think you're not ready? Did you have another episode today?"

She shook her head. "No, I think it's just too much on me right now. I need to get a better grip on myself first." She turned and looked up at me. "Let's not talk about it tonight. I want to cook you dinner and enjoy being with you."

I tucked my head in the curve of her neck. "Okay," I replied. We would talk about it tomorrow then. "How can I help you with dinner?"

She turned and kissed my head. "You can slice the French bread, butter it, then sprinkle it with garlic powder. I need to toast it."

"I can do that," I said, stepping back from Della and reaching for the bread.

Della

I had known deep down that this wouldn't be forever. I'd thought once Woods realized how impossible life would be with me that he would end it. But that wasn't true. He was already tired of dealing with my being "crazy," but he'd never let me know. He made me feel cherished. If I hadn't heard him talking to Jace I would still have been holding on to the belief that we could work through it all.

Years of not living among other people had hindered my ability to read them. Jace had known that Woods was tired of dealing with me but I hadn't gotten the hint. I knew now. Tonight would be it for us. I had cooked for him and enjoyed looking at him and listening to him talk. I wanted to etch every moment of tonight in my memory.

When I left tomorrow, that would be it. I wasn't coming back and Woods would be relieved. At first he would be upset. I thought he loved me. I was just more than he'd bargained for. When he realized I'd taken myself out of the picture for him, his life would get easier. He could be free of worrying about me.

Tonight, though, he was still mine. I could hold him and believe in what we had. Just once more.

We stood side by side and cleaned up the dishes. Normally

we talked and laughed but I couldn't find anything fun to talk about. My heart was too heavy.

"Are you okay?" Woods asked when he put the last dish in the dishwasher and closed it.

I nodded and smiled.

He reached over and laced his fingers through mine. "Are you sure? I'll fix whatever is wrong if you just tell me," he said, gently tugging me to him. He was a fixer. He wanted to fix my life, and that wasn't possible.

Instead of answering, I stood up on my tiptoes and pressed my lips to his neck. "I want you," I whispered against his warm skin. "Right now, all I want is you."

Woods let me kiss down his neck, and when I tugged at his T-shirt he lifted his arms and let me take it off. His chiseled chest was always tanned and perfect. I ran my fingers over the beautiful skin and each hard ab muscle that fascinated me. This had been mine for a time. It would be a chapter in my life that was hard to look back on, yet it would be my favorite.

I pressed my lips to the taut skin of his lower stomach and started undoing his jeans. He stood there and let me. I was glad there was no resistance or questions. If we were ending this chapter tonight, I wanted it to be perfect.

I pulled his jeans down with his boxer briefs.

"Fuck, Della," he whispered as I licked the tip of his cock. Both of his hands were now buried in my hair as I lowered myself to my knees in front of him. I wanted him to know I loved him. When I was gone I wanted him to know that he was a part of me. That this hadn't been empty for me.

"Oh, hell," he groaned, leaning back against the counter for support as I sank his length into my mouth until it slid into my throat. I loved the way this made him feel. Knowing the trembling in his legs was because of me was a wonderful feeling. He made me tremble all the time. I liked making him tremble in return.

"That's so damn good, baby. Your hot little mouth is fucking perfect." His voice was husky and deep. I reached up and cupped his balls in my hand. He let out a low growl and suddenly I was being jerked up. "Not gonna come in your mouth. Not tonight. I want inside you," he said, kicking off his jeans and leaving them on the floor before picking me up and walking to the bedroom.

His hands were on my shorts, jerking them off. I raised my arms and let him pull my top off. My bra and panties went just as quickly.

"You're beautiful," he said as he knelt above me and stared down at my body.

When I was with him I felt beautiful. "Make love to me," I told him as I opened my thighs and reached up to pull him down to me.

"I want to taste you," he said, stopping me from pulling him down farther.

"I want you inside me," I replied.

"Don't care. I want a taste first." His crooked grin warmed my heart. I'd let him have whatever he wanted.

"Okay," I replied as he lowered himself until his head was between my thighs.

His lips brushed the sensitive skin on the insides of my legs as he trailed kisses, switching from one leg to the other until the heat of his breath touched my tender flesh. I shuddered and grabbed handfuls of the sheets underneath me just before his tongue slipped inside of me and then moved up to my clit.

I cried out his name until I came against his mouth. Every single flick of his tongue had taken me farther under the wave of pleasure that overtook me.

As I gasped to get air into my lungs, he filled me in one swift move. I lifted my knees and pressed them to his ribs. "I love you, Della. I love you so much, baby. So damn much," he said with a hoarse voice full of emotion. It was as if he knew this was it for us. That tomorrow wouldn't come. This was the end. I fought back the tears clogging my throat and grabbed his face so that I could kiss him. I couldn't talk. I didn't trust myself to talk. I showed him how much I loved him with my mouth.

With each thrust I lifted my knees and cried out. He never stopped telling me how much he loved me. It was a chant as we both climbed to our release.

"*Woods!*" I screamed his name in ecstasy as the world blurred.

He held me to his chest as he jerked inside of me. My name was a strangled cry from his chest as he shuddered against me.

Our chapter was over. It was the most beautiful chapter in my life. I knew I'd had the happy ending way before it was time and now I had to live the rest of the story without him. It wasn't the way life was supposed to be, but it was my life. And I'd had Woods in it. That made it all okay.

◇

Woods had kissed my head, telling me to sleep late. He had an early meeting and I could come to work when I was ready. I had pretended to be sleepy and nodded, keeping my head buried in the pillow to hide my tears. When the door clicked behind him I turned over and stared at the ceiling.

My heart had just walked out that door.

I moved without thought as I showered and dressed. I boxed up the things I would be shipping that morning to the address Tripp had texted me. I then packed a small bag I could carry with me. I wasn't sure where we were going and when we would make it back to the South Carolina address I was shipping my things to.

Woods called me around ten and asked if I wanted to eat lunch with him. I didn't want to lie to him but I couldn't tell him the truth either. So I told him I was behind on work and if he wanted me to come back, then I needed to catch up. He didn't argue with me. When I told him that I loved him one tear rolled down my face. I was glad he couldn't see me.

On a piece of paper I wrote:

I will never forget you. Thank you for everything but it's time I move on. I want to see the world. This life isn't for me. It doesn't fit. It isn't what I dreamed of. Don't come after me, just let me go. I hope you find the happiness you deserve.

I'm sorry,
Della

Woods

I ended the strange phone call from Tripp and stared down at my phone for a few minutes. Nothing about that conversation had made sense. He'd asked me how life was. I'd told him it was good. He had said I should strive for great. I told him it was perfect and he had gone silent. Then he'd said, *Sometimes what we think is perfect is royally fucked up.* I had asked him what he meant and he said he was just checking in and hoped I'd figure life out soon.

What the hell had all that meant? Was he drinking before lunch? Glancing at my clock, I realized it was my tee time with Jace. When Della had turned me down for lunch I'd let her because she wanted to work. I couldn't keep making her feel like she wasn't important. So to keep myself from begging her to have lunch with me, I'd called Jace and set up a tee time for us.

I had a meeting with my new lawyer at three, then after that I would hunt her down. I thought she'd be ready to take a break then. Smiling, I let Tripp's weird phone call go and I headed down to the golf course.

Jace was standing at Bethy's golf cart with his hands on the roof as he leaned in, flirting with her. I never would have guessed those two would have made it so long. Bethy had been the wild local girl who lived in the next town over. She slept with the rich boys and they acted like they didn't know her in public. Until Jace. He'd decided that she was worth it. He had seen something more.

"You gonna stop making out with my employee long enough to play a round?" I asked as I approached them.

Jace grinned over at me, then flipped his middle finger. "Suck it, Kerrington."

"You two need me to get y'all a caddy?" Bethy asked.

"We're real men, baby. We don't need a caddy," Jace said, winking at her.

"Let's do this. I have a three o'clock appointment," I informed Jace.

The cart I'd ordered was brought around with my clubs. Jace said his good-byes to Bethy and put his clubs in the back of the cart. "It's been a while since we played a round," Jace said. "Boss man never has any time."

"Della has taken a lot off me. I need to give her a raise."

Jace chuckled and propped his feet up on the dash of the cart. "You told your momma about the new-board idea?"

"I won't be telling her. It isn't her business. I'm meeting with the lawyer today to make sure this is handled the correct way. The lawyer will make sure the board knows they've been terminated."

"You know, I always thought the board, like, owned a portion of the club," Jace said.

"My grandfather forbade it in his will. He wanted the club to always be under the Kerrington name. He didn't allow investors unless they were family. That was one of the reasons my father wanted me to marry Angelina. She would become family and he would merge her father's clubs with the Kerrington Club. My grandfather wouldn't have wanted that. I've looked over his business plan. I know his dream for this place. My father had other ideas and he was going to use me to accomplish them."

Jace let out a low whistle as we pulled up to the first tee. "Damn, no wonder your dad was ready to marry you off to a psycho. So, you really own it all now. You make the decisions. That board was just so your father had people to help him build and make decisions."

"I think he had promised them a piece of the pie once the Kerrington Club was part of the Greystone empire. Everything would have changed then. He also paid them well. I looked over the payroll."

Jace jumped out and pulled his driver from the bag before heading over to the tee. "So you're saying I'm gonna get a nice fat paycheck for being on this new board," Jace drawled.

"Yeah, that's what I'm saying," I replied, pulling the driver from my bag.

"Good. Because I'm gonna propose to Bethy and my family is gonna shit a brick. I can kiss my monthly income good-bye. I need to start using this education my father paid so handsomely for."

I stopped walking. Had I just heard him right? "Did you just say *propose*?"

Jace looked up from his stance over the ball and nodded.

"Wow," was all I could think of to say. I hadn't expected that.

"I love her. She's it for me."

I stood there silently as Jace hit the ball. He stepped back and glanced over at me. "She doesn't know yet. I'm trying to think of a romantic way to do it."

This golf game had just gotten a lot more interesting.

◇

I texted Della before my three o'clock meeting but she didn't respond before the lawyer arrived. Once my meeting was over and there was still no response, I dialed her number. I hadn't seen her all day. Neither had anyone I asked. Something felt wrong.

"I'm sorry, but the number you have dialed has been disconnected . . ." I jerked my phone back and looked down to make sure I'd dialed Della's number. I had.

I grabbed my keys and walked past Vince without a word. My mind was running wild. Why would Della's phone be disconnected? Had she forgotten to pay the bill? Was she okay?

As I got to the house, every bad scenario ran through my head. The car I'd given Della when she'd come back to Rosemary with me was sitting in the drive. She hadn't left the house today. My heart raced as I ran up the steps and swung the door open.

It was quiet. Too quiet.

"Della? Baby? You okay?" I called out as I walked down the hall toward the living room. I glanced into the kitchen as I passed and almost continued on when I saw a single piece of paper and a pen lying on the counter. They hadn't been there that morning.

"Della?" I called out again, walking on toward the living room and out onto the balcony. The bedroom was empty. It was also bare. There were no heels lying by the door or jewelry on the dresser. I stood in the doorway, afraid to walk inside and look in the closet.

I turned and headed back to the kitchen. The note would explain this. She could have cleaned up before she went shopping with Blaire. That made sense.

Reaching for the paper, I picked it up and began to read. With each word, my world began to slowly fall away. The small, ripped piece of notebook paper held the only words that could completely destroy me.

I let it fall to the floor as I stood frozen. I didn't want to touch it. I didn't want to see it. The words were imprinted in my head. I'd never be able to make them go away. I couldn't move. I couldn't breathe.

Della

Tripp hadn't said much when he came to get me. He had just asked if I was sure, and when I'd said yes he had taken my bag and put it in the compartment of his bike before handing me a helmet and a leather jacket. I put both on.

We had been riding for about two hours when he pulled into a gas station. My legs were slightly numb. I wasn't sure I could walk when I got off that thing. Tripp got off and then took my helmet and hung it on the bike. I didn't ask him why he wasn't wearing a helmet but I was glad he had one for me to wear. He then held his hand out to help me off. I managed to sling my leg over the bike and held on to both his hands as I stood up.

"Ouch," I said with a weak smile.

He grinned. "Yeah, you'll get used to it," he told me, then nodded his head toward the store. "Go in, use the restroom, and get yourself something to eat and drink. We'll take a little break before we go any farther."

I had focused on the road and the cars we passed. I'd managed to fight off any thoughts of Woods. But they were there in my head, teasing me. They wanted to haunt me. They wanted to break me. He would know soon that I was gone. "Where are we going?" I asked, trying to think of anything other than Woods.

82

"Not sure. We're just riding. I thought you might need that right now. I'm heading north. I figure we'll find somewhere interesting by bedtime to stop at."

This was what I needed. I nodded. "Okay."

"I gotta fill up," he told me, and I headed inside the store. I would need to call Braden now. I hadn't told her I was leaving Woods. She wouldn't have seen it my way. But once Woods knew I was gone he would call her first. She would be worried. I should prepare her. I slipped my phone out of my pocket and remembered I'd had it switched off. I didn't want to be traceable. I would reactivate it in the next big city. A new number. One no one knew.

After using the restroom I grabbed a bottle of water and some Cheetos, paid, and headed outside to sit at a picnic table that sat in a grassy area.

Tripp glanced over at me before he went inside and did the same. By the time he came outside I was finished with my bag of Cheetos. He dropped a candy bar, a bag of peanuts, some beef jerky, and a bag of gummy worms on the table. "Eat some more," he said before picking up the beef jerky and taking a bite of it.

I reached for the candy bar and broke it in half before eating it. We ate in silence. I was afraid to try to talk to him. He wanted to know why I was doing this. He didn't think I should. I could tell by the way he was acting.

"He didn't know you were leaving. Didn't even have a clue. That sucks, Della. It really does. The dude's gonna take this real hard."

I stopped eating and stood up. "I can't think about that right now, okay? I need to think about other things. Not that. It's what was best for him. That's all I can tell you. Please, let's not talk about it."

Tripp let out a weary sigh, then nodded. "Fine. We won't talk about it. Not right now, anyway. Eat some worms, they're good for you," he said with a smirk as he pushed the bag of gummy worms toward me.

"I'm not hungry." I wasn't. I felt sick now.

"Fine. I'll take this with us. You'll get hungry again soon. You barely ate anything."

"Can I use your phone to call my friend Braden?"

Tripp nodded and pulled his phone out of his pocket to hand it to me.

"Thanks," I replied as I took it from him.

I walked far enough away that he wouldn't hear me. I was going to lie to Braden some, if only to keep her from telling Woods the truth.

Dialing her number, I held my breath, hoping that I could find a way to tell her and make it believable. She would go straight to Woods with my location and reason for leaving if she knew the truth.

"Hello?" Braden's voice sounded curious. She didn't recognize the number.

"It's me," I said into the phone.

"Della? Where are you?"

"I'm traveling the world. Living life. Woods's life isn't what I want for myself. I need adventure."

Braden didn't respond. She was thinking. I knew the look on her face even though I couldn't see it.

"What happened? Stop bullshitting me and tell me where you are and what's wrong." I was a horrible liar and Braden knew me better than anyone.

"I'm traveling. I'm not alone and I'm okay. I just need some time. I'll check in when I can but I need time to move on from things. This is why I got in your car and took off to begin with, anyway. Woods changed that but it was only temporary. I need to do this for me."

"I'm still calling bullshit. I don't believe you but I won't push. Call me when you can, and be safe. Can I trust who you're with to keep you safe?"

"Yes," I replied.

"You won't tell me who it is?"

"No. I need you to not tell Woods that you talked to me. Tell him nothing. He will come after me and I don't want him to."

Braden let out a small growl of frustration. "He loves you, Della," she said.

"And I love him. But it's time I lived. I can't be locked up in that small town."

"I hope you're not making the biggest mistake of your life," she said in a defeated tone.

"It was the best chapter. I'll have more chapters though."

"I love you," Braden said.

"I love you, too," I replied.

"Call me soon."

"I will."

I hung up and walked back over to Tripp, who was watching me.

"Thanks," I said, handing back his phone.

"Did you have yours turned off so he couldn't track you?" he asked, standing up.

I nodded.

"Damn, girl. You didn't leave the boy a bone, did you?"

"Can we go? I just want to ride."

"Yeah, let's go," he said, and headed for the Harley parked near the table.

Woods

She hadn't left me anything but a note. She'd taken all her things. I held the pillow she'd slept on last night and pressed my face to it. It smelled like her. The sexy sweet scent that was Della.

How was I supposed to let her go? She didn't want me to find her . . . she wanted to live. This wasn't living for her. She had started out on a journey to see the world and she'd met me. Now she wanted more.

I'd hovered over her. I had tried to keep her safe and not let her do things she wanted. I'd controlled her job and what she did. She wanted to spread her wings and I'd clipped them. So she'd found another way to fly.

My chest was so tight that each breath I took was painful. I hadn't called anyone. I hadn't left my house for hours. I held the pillow closer and glanced over at the clock. It was after nine. I'd been home for five hours. How long had she been gone? Had she known last night that she was leaving me?

The look in her eyes as she'd made love to me had been different. There had been something in them that bothered me. But she had been so passionate and needy that I'd forgotten about everything other than the pleasure. If I had just looked deeper and talked to her . . . Instead, it had been about sex. When she had fallen to her knees in the kitchen, I was lost to whatever she wanted.

If I'd only looked deeper.

How had she left me?

Slowly, a realization came to me and I stood up, still holding her pillow. The phone call from Tripp. He hadn't made sense but he'd been trying to tell me. *Motherfucker!* She'd left with Tripp. She had called him and he had come for her.

The pain slowly started heating up as anger—no, fury— consumed me. She had left with Tripp. He had taken her from me. His call wouldn't have made sense to anyone. It had been his way of being able to say he had warned me when he knew I wouldn't understand him.

I reached for the lamp on the bedside table and threw it against the wall. Then I threw the sheets and shoved over the nightstand. I grabbed the mirror off the wall and smashed it, but the anger was still there. I punched the wall until my fist went through the Sheetrock and my voice seemed so far away, even though I was yelling. I had stepped outside of myself as my body went mad. Then I threw the pillow in my hand and everything stopped. That was all I had. Her pillow. I walked over to the pile of broken glass and furniture and picked the pillow back up. I held it reverently to my chest.

Her scent filled my senses and for a moment the fury eased. For a moment I wasn't a hysterical madman bent on demolishing everything in my house. I had her. I could hold this. I had her.

"Holy shit." Jace's voice came from the doorway. I snapped my head up to see him looking into my room. The horrified look on his face as he lifted his eyes to me only made me angry again.

"Dude," he said, holding up both his hands. "You gotta calm down."

He didn't understand. He hadn't just lost his reason for fucking living. She hadn't just walked away from him. Left him nothing but a note and a pillow. The note . . . shit.

I stalked to the door and shoved past Jace. I had to get the note. I had the note, too. It was something of hers. I had that. I wanted it. Even if the words in it tore me wide open, I wanted it.

The torn paper lay on the floor and I scrambled to pick it up. I couldn't read the words again. Not right now. I folded it carefully and tucked it into my pocket. I'd keep it on me. This was her handwriting. Her words.

"You're scaring me, man." Jace had followed me to the kitchen.

"I need to be alone," I said without turning to look at him.

"I don't think you need to be alone."

"Leave my motherfucking house," I snarled.

"I've called Rush and Thad. They're on their way. I'm not leaving you alone."

I didn't want them here. I wanted to yell and break things. I wanted to find a way to ease the pain. "No! Why are you even here?"

"Tripp called me," he said slowly. Just hearing his name and knowing that he was the one who had Della made the monster inside of me snap. I reached for the glass in the sink and threw it across the room, shattering a picture.

"He took her!" I roared as I grabbed a plate and hurled it across the room. "He fucking took her from me!"

"She called him. She wanted to go with him, Woods. You

gotta calm down. She left of her own free will." I could hear
the fear in Jace's voice but I didn't care. I grabbed a bar stool
and began smashing it against the counter until the wood shat-
tered into pieces in a heap on the floor.

"Holy hell." Rush's voice registered in my brain but I
couldn't think. I didn't want them there.

"Dude! Stop him. He's gone fucking mad," Thad said.

Arms wrapped around me from behind and I fought against
them, but they held me tighter. "Chill the fuck out. Breathe,
man. Fucking take a breath. She isn't dead. She left. She's out
there and it ain't over. So calm the fuck down," Rush said in a
stern, loud voice as he held my arms back.

I took several deep breaths. He was right. She was alive.
She had just left. She had left. "She left me," I said, and my
voice broke.

"Yeah, she did. But you can't beat the hell out of your house.
It won't bring her back and you're getting out of control. Get
it together. I know what this feels like. I've been there. Losing
your shit doesn't make her come back to you."

Rush had been here. He knew. Blaire had left him once. But
she'd been betrayed. She'd had a reason to. I hadn't hurt Della.
I had only loved her.

"I didn't let her live," I said, lifting my eyes to look straight
ahead at Jace and Thad, who were keeping their distance
from me.

"She needs some space. Let her have it," Rush said.

"How do I keep going? With her gone? What do I do?"

Rush let out a sigh and slowly let his hold on me go. "You
wake up each morning and you go to work. You smile when
you think you're supposed to. You spend your free time think-

ing about her. Thinking about what you'll say when you see her again. Then you go to bed and hope you get some sleep. Then you wake up and do that same shit over again."

I leaned against the wall and hung my head. "What if she never comes back?" He didn't say anything at first. We stood there in silence among the destruction.

"Then you find a way to keep living," Rush finally said, and I realized that was my biggest fear. That I'd be left needing to find a way, because Della might never come back.

"She was my go-all-in," I said as I stared down at the smashed-up bar stool.

"Your what?" Jace asked.

"Della was my go-all-in. She was my winning hand. You can't play when you go all in and lose. I'm out."

"No, you're not. This hand ain't over yet," Rush said.

I hoped he was right.

Two weeks later

Della

"Where are we now?" I asked Tripp as I got off the back of his bike—without his help this time.

"What have you been doing back there? Sleeping? We've passed several signs announcing our arrival at the home of the King," Tripp said as he grabbed our bags and headed for the hotel to get us a room.

"The King?" I asked, following him.

"Yeah, you know . . . hunka hunka burnin' love," Tripp said.

"Elvis? You mean we're in Memphis?"

"Yep," Tripp said as he pushed open the door to the hotel and held it for me so I could go inside. Our first night I had tried to stay in my own room, but the night terrors had come fast and hard. Since then, we got rooms with two beds and Tripp helped me when the dreams came, which was every night so far. We were both so tired this week that most nights we ended up falling asleep in the same bed once the terror was over, sleeping that way through the rest of the night.

"One room, two beds," Tripp told the lady, and she glanced

over at me, then back at Tripp and flashed him a flirty smile. He got that a lot. When females realized we weren't together they started throwing themselves at him. He ignored it for the most part. Sometimes there would be a girl he couldn't ignore. He would flirt back and take her number, which I thought was pointless since we weren't coming back. But he said he might just come back one day.

Tripp got the key to our room and we headed to the elevator. I didn't feel like talking much. I had called Braden earlier and she'd told me that Woods still hadn't called her. That bothered me. I should have been relieved. But I wasn't. The longer I was away from him without his calling Tripp or Braden, the more I realized this was what he wanted. Deep down, I'd given him his out. I didn't want to think about his being in pain. It made it easier to function each day knowing that the never-ending ache in my heart was something I suffered alone.

"You're quiet today," Tripp said as the elevator door opened and we stepped out onto the second floor. That was as high as Tripp would go. He had a thing about being too high up in a hotel. He said that if the place caught on fire he wanted to know he didn't have too many flights of stairs to take to get the hell out. I hadn't really thought about it but he had, apparently.

"Just not in the mood to talk," I told him.

"Your talk with Braden go okay?" he asked.

Sure. It had gone fine. She hadn't brought up Woods. She had only asked me where we had gone and what we were doing. Nothing more. "Yeah, it was fine."

Tripp opened the door to our room and glanced back at me. "You okay if I go out and get a drink tonight?"

This was code for "You okay if I go out and get laid tonight?" He didn't know that I had this figured out and I preferred that we keep it that way.

Every night he went out for a drink he came back around two in the morning smelling like perfume. He would have made a horrible cheating husband.

"I want to order a pizza and watch cable. Go, do what you want," I told him as I walked into the room.

"Thanks," he said, stepping in behind me.

"No problem. I need a shower. You leaving now?" I asked, taking my bag from his hands and heading for the bathroom.

"Yeah, I think so."

"See you in the morning," I told him. I stepped into the bathroom and closed the door behind me. I waited until I heard the hotel room door close and he had sufficient time to get away before I let the tears come. I'd been holding them back for hours. Crying didn't make the pain easier, but for that one moment I could lose myself in my sorrow. I didn't have to hide it. I could let it out freely.

Deep down, I knew what I had done was right. I'd let Woods go. My fear that I would hurt him no longer haunted me. He was okay. He was living his life and he would find that someone who could be his perfect fit. What we'd had was never going to be perfect. Love should be simple. I wasn't simple.

Woods deserved someone like Blaire Finlay. He needed a woman by his side who could pull out a gun and take care of herself. A wife who could give him babies that he could love and know they would be mentally healthy. The fear that their mother could snap would never be there.

I would never be a Blaire. I wanted to be more than I wanted my next breath, but it would never happen. I wasn't Woods's simple perfection. He would find it one day with someone else. Maybe one day I would find a way to be happy again. Maybe living life would help me find my place.

I refused to believe I would end up damaged like my mother. I might not have been wife-and-mother material, but I was a person. I could be something. I could make a difference in this world. I just had to find out what that something was. Thinking about Woods and his disinterest in finding me wasn't doing me any good. Crying wasn't healing me.

It was time I healed myself. I didn't need a man to hold my hand and cuddle me. I needed to do this on my own. Woods had wanted to help me and I'd wanted someone to cling to.

Tripp and I had pooled our money together and it had been enough for a while, but it wouldn't last forever. It was time Tripp went back to his place in South Carolina and I found a life. One that I lived alone. One in which I depended on myself.

I stood up and turned on the shower and undressed. I would wash away my tears and I wouldn't allow myself to do this again. There was a bravery inside of me that I was going to find and nurture.

Woods

I sat outside on my balcony with a beer in one hand and my phone in the other. Tripp called at nine every night. It was the only way I kept myself sane. Listening to him tell me about what she was doing, what she was saying, and even what she was wearing was the only way I held on to my last shreds of sanity.

The moment Tripp's name lit up the screen I answered.

"Hey, how is she?" I didn't care about small talk. I had decided not to find Tripp and break all the limbs from his body when he'd called me the first time and promised to keep me updated on Della. He said she needed time to deal with things and I needed to give her that. I was trying like hell but I wanted to go to her. Every time he told me which city they were in, I fought the need to jump on a plane.

"She was quiet today. Didn't talk much and couldn't wait to get rid of me. She's depressed but this is just another stage for her."

"Where are you now?"

"Memphis."

"Are you checked into a hotel?"

"Yeah. She's in the room. I'm out, giving her some space tonight."

Giving her space? Alone, in a strange city? "What the fuck are you thinking? You can't leave her alone! If she's been quiet she may be closing in on herself. You can't leave her alone. She'll need someone to bring her back. She can't—"

"Woods! Calm down, man. Calm down." Tripp's voice was commanding.

"She can't be alone," I said again as emotion lodged in my throat. I hated to think of her alone.

"She needs to be alone. She needs to cry. She needs to decide if giving you this freedom she thinks you need is going to be possible. Her leaving is all about you, Woods. She didn't want to leave you. I've told you that already. She loves you so much that she left to give you the life she thinks you want. One where you don't have to deal with her shit. So, now that she's done that, she has to live with it. Give her time. She'll come back."

I had set my beer down and stood up. Gripping the railing, I closed my eyes and fought back the pain. I just wanted her. Just Della. Any way I could have her, I wanted her. I wasn't ever going to be all right. I didn't want her to be alone. I wanted someone to hold her.

"Hold her for me. Hold her tight. Don't let her be lonely. Don't let her hurt. Please."

"I will do what she allows me to do. But my arms aren't the ones she wants."

"Fuck," I growled as sharp pains wrapped around my throat.

"Just give her more time," Tripp said.

I took several long, steadying breaths. He had to get back to her. He couldn't leave her alone like this. "When we hang up, go back to her."

Tripp sighed. "Fine. But I had plans tonight. There's a hot little bartender giving me the eye."

"Do you need more money?" I asked him. I had been depositing money into his account since he had called the first night. I wanted her in nice hotels and I wanted her to eat well.

"She's going to notice soon that we aren't running out of money. I keep waiting for her to bring up the fact that we stay in the nicest part of each town and eat in high-end restaurants instead of fast-food chains. She's not an idiot."

"I'm holding on by a damn thread. Your phone calls and the fact I know she's in nice hotels and eating good food is the only fucking thing keeping me sane."

"I'm going to see if I can convince her to go back to my place in South Carolina with me. I have a nice place there. It's safe and I have a job I can go back to. I can get her a job, too."

I just wanted her to come home. "Whatever you need to do. But she stays safe."

"I'm keeping her safe. I promise."

"You took her from me," I reminded him. I couldn't thank him.

"She asked me to. I'm her friend, too."

"She needs me."

"No, dude. Right now, she needs to find the strength inside herself. The strength she doesn't think is there. Once she realizes that she isn't a burden, she'll be back."

"She has to," I said, then ended the call before Tripp heard the pain in my voice.

Della

The pizza hadn't even arrived yet when Tripp walked back in the door. I had been sure he was going to screw a stranger. "You're back?"

He shrugged. "I decided I'd rather have pizza instead of a beer."

Something was up. He wouldn't rather have had pizza than get laid. Tripp was a bit of a man-whore. I had figured this out pretty fast. Women liked him and he liked them right back—for about two or three hours, then he was gone.

"Why are you really back? You never choose pizza over . . . beer."

A crooked grin tugged at his lips and he shifted his gaze over to me. "By the way you just said *beer*, I'm going to assume you know what I'm normally up to when I step out for a drink."

I rolled my eyes. "Uh, yeah."

Tripp sank down on the edge of the other bed. "Well, tonight I was thinking about something and I thought we might need to talk more than I needed a beer."

I wasn't sure how to respond to that so I just waited.

The knock on the door stopped him from going any farther.

"Pizza," he said, standing up and going to pay for the pizza. I had also ordered a two-liter soda. It wasn't beer but it came with the special.

I watched as he set the pizza down on my bed and grabbed the two plastic glasses by the ice bucket and fixed us a drink. I had been thinking we needed to talk, too, I just wasn't sure when we would get the chance. Before we got any farther away from South Carolina, I planned on telling him we should go there.

"Meat lover's. It's like you knew I was coming back," he said.

"No. The special tonight was a large meat lover's and a two-liter soda for fifteen dollars. I went with the special."

"Lucky me," he replied.

"Talk, Tripp. I want to know what's more important than beer."

Tripp let out a small chuckle and took a drink of his soda. Then he settled his green eyes on me. "Impatient, aren't you."

I didn't reply. I just raised my eyebrows to let him know I was still waiting.

"We need to go back to South Carolina. I need to get back to my job and I can get you hooked up with a job, too. I have a place there and it will be good for you to stay in one place longer than a day and think about stuff."

Not what I had been expecting him to say.

"Okay," I replied.

He stopped chewing. "'Okay'? Just like that?"

I nodded. "Yeah, just like that."

He finished chewing his bite of pizza and swallowed. "Why do you always surprise me? All the damn time? You'd think I would be used to it by now."

I took another bite of my pizza and shrugged. I hadn't realized I was going to be so easygoing about it either. I wasn't going to stay there permanently, of course, but I could work there awhile and save up some money. Then I would hit the road again.

"There is one thing I want to do first," I told him.

"What?"

"Go through Georgia and see my best friend, Braden, and her husband, Kent. I haven't seen them in a while and I'd like to stay at their house for a couple of days."

Tripp nodded. "Sounds good. I can get a place at a hotel in town and you can stay with them."

"They would be happy for you to stay with them, too," I assured him.

Tripp smirked. "Yeah, well, that sounds nice but honestly, I could really use a couple of nights to have some . . . beer."

The small bubble of laughter was fast and unexpected. Tripp's smirk turned into a pleased grin, and I laughed for the first time since I'd left Rosemary.

⟡

Later that night, I had just started to fall asleep when I heard Tripp get up and walk to the bathroom. I thought he was going to take a shower but I heard him talking to someone. Who would he be calling after midnight? Then I heard my name.

I eased out of bed quietly and tiptoed close enough so I could hear what he was saying.

"She wants to stop by her friend's house in Georgia first. . . . Yeah. . . . I said yes. Damn. . . . Near Myrtle Beach. It's safe. I swear. . . . Probably need some more, yeah. . . . I'll call you. . . . I said I would call you. Go to sleep."

I hurried back over to the bed and crawled back in. Whom had he been talking to? Was there a girl back where he lived? Had he left someone behind to come help me? No. That couldn't be it. He slept with too many women. Maybe it was just a friend.

"Della?" Tripp's voice surprised me and I almost responded. Then I realized he was checking to make sure I was asleep. I didn't say anything.

It must have been a friend of his wondering when he'd be home. But the "safe" comment—that was weird. I closed my eyes and decided to let the exhaustion take me. I would think about this tomorrow.

Woods

I stared down at the list of appointments that Vince had put on my desk that morning. I had been putting off so much shit because I couldn't focus in the last two weeks, and now I was behind. Tomorrow my lawyer would be sending out the letters to the former board members letting them know that they were no longer needed. I expected the shit to hit the fan but I was letting my lawyer deal with the blows. I wasn't in the mood for it.

"Mr. Finlay here to see you, sir," Vince's voice said over the intercom.

"Send him in," I replied. I had called Rush's father, Dean Finlay, before Della had left. I figured if I put someone on the board who was a celebrity, then it would help with the members and the town when they heard of the new board. Besides, Dean had put a lot of money into the Kerrington Club and my father had never approved of him. He'd acknowledged him because he wasn't a complete fool but he hadn't liked him.

"I gotta say, Woods, you look pretty goddamn good sitting in that seat," Dean drawled as he sauntered into the room. He reeked of rock star, from his long hair to his tattoo-covered body and many piercings. He even had on eyeliner. The man was a legend and I had grown up with him as the father of one of my friends.

"Thanks, Dean," I said, standing up and reaching across the desk to shake his hand.

"You got me for about thirty minutes. Then I'm gonna have to get back to that grandson of mine. I had to leave him all giggly and playful and that's pretty fucking hard to do. The kid's adorable."

"Yes, sir. I will make this quick," I assured him, and motioned for him to sit down.

Dean sat down in the leather wingback chair and propped his feet up on the edge of my desk. "What's up?"

"I'm letting my father's board members go. They were close confidants of my father; however, I don't feel the same way about them. I have no need for a board that I can't share my ideas with and whose opinions I can't trust. I'm replacing the board with people I want to have input into the future of the Kerrington Club."

Dean held up a hand to stop me, then he cocked one dark eyebrow. "Are you saying you fired all their uppity asses?"

I nodded.

Dean threw his head back and cackled with laughter. "Damn, that's the funniest shit I've heard in a while."

If I could have managed a smile these days I would have smiled then. "I want you on my board, sir. Rush will also be asked, of course."

Dean dropped his feet to the floor and leaned forward, resting his elbows on his knees, and studied me a moment. "You want me on your board?"

"Yes, I do. My group of friends are all young. We need wisdom on the board and you're the only man I know that I would want advising me."

A slow smile spread across Dean's face. "I'll be damned."

Probably, but I wasn't going to agree with him. I just waited.

"Hell yeah, I'll be on your board. My grandson is going to grow up in this town and the Kerrington Club and the members here will be a big part of his life. I want to make sure he has the best."

I had hoped he would feel that way. "Thank you, sir. I appreciate it. I'm honored that you will be a part of the future of the club."

"Me too," he said, leaning back in his chair. "But, Woods, if we're gonna do this, then should you stop calling me *sir*. Makes me sound old. I bang chicks younger than you, son."

I might not have been able to smile but I was amused. "I'm sure you do," I replied.

"That was pretty damn funny. What's wrong with you, boy? I can't seem to get you to crack a smile."

I didn't want to talk about Della with Dean. He wouldn't understand. Like he said, he was with a different girl every night. "Personal stuff. I'm working through it."

Dean rubbed his chin, then tilted his head as he looked at me too closely. "It's a woman. That look is always caused by a fucking woman. Don't bother denying it. I can see it all over your face."

I didn't admit it but I didn't deny it. Instead, I dropped my eyes to the table and shifted through some paperwork. I had a contract Dean needed to sign and we needed to discuss his monthly salary, not that he needed it.

"Who is she? What did she do? She getting under your

skin and you're ready to run, or has she already got you on her hook and she's trying to let you go?"

I pulled out the contract and took my pen and pushed them across the table. "Neither. I need you to sign the contract saying everything we discuss about the club is confidential. Your salary is listed as well."

Dean didn't lean forward and take the paper. He was still focused on me. He started to shake his head and let out a low whistle. "Woods motherfucking Kerrington is in love. Damn, it's in the water down here. I need to get my ass back to LA. You young boys going manic over one pretty little girl. There's lots of fish. Lots of fucking beautiful fish. Why worry about one when you can have 'em all? Brunette on Monday and a redhead on Tuesday, twins on Wednesday, a blonde with big ole titties on Thursday, an Asian beauty on Friday, and her sister on Saturday, then on Sunday is when you get you one of each and have one big-ass party all damn day. No need to get wrapped up in just one."

This was very similar to a speech he'd given us one summer when Rush had taken us on a road trip to see Slacker Demon in Atlanta. We had, of course, been granted backstage access and hung out with the band. It was Dean's life. I had thought it was a lonely life back then. Now that I'd had Della, I knew it was a lonely life. I wasn't interested.

"Just want the one," I told him.

"She must be special," he said, and leaned forward to pick up the pen. "I'm not signing my life away or adding you to my will, am I?" he asked.

"No, just agreeing to keep the club's business confidential."

"I don't need the money. Put it in a trust fund for Nate. Have Rush set it up."

I'd expected as much. "Yes, sir"—his head snapped up—"I mean, Dean," I said, correcting myself.

He nodded. "Better." Then he stood up and slapped his hand down on the desk. "Looks good on you, boy. Looks real good on you," he said, then turned and walked out of the office.

I had Dean. Now I needed to make my next call.

Della

Braden threw open the door and wrapped her arms around me in one swift movement. I dropped the bag I was carrying and hugged her back just as fiercely.

"You're here! I missed you," Braden said as she squeezed me one more time, then pulled back and glanced over at Tripp. I didn't miss the appreciative gleam in Tripp's eyes as he took in my best friend. Braden had big, round, cornflower-blue eyes and long, dark curly lashes. Her brown curls were completely natural. I had been coveting them for years.

"Braden, this is my friend Tripp. Tripp, this is my best friend, Braden Fredrick."

"And I'm her husband, Kent," Kent said as he walked up behind Braden. I smiled over at him. I felt like I should apologize for Tripp and I was suddenly glad he was going to stay in a hotel. Braden loved her husband but when Tripp wanted to be a charmer he had it down to a science.

"It's nice to meet both of you," Tripp said with a knowing smile. I should probably have pinched him.

"Y'all come on in," Braden said, stepping back.

"I have plans this evening so I need to head on out. I'll be back when you're ready to leave, Della," he said, and winked at me. He was being cute on purpose.

"Okay. Go drink beer. I think you need it," I told him, and he laughed before turning and going back to his bike.

"He drives a Harley?" Braden asked, peering at him as he walked away.

"Stop it before Kent goes out there and tries to beat him up," I whispered, and stepped inside, letting the door close behind me.

"What? Kent knows I love him. I was just looking. I'm curious about who you've been riding all over the place with these past two weeks."

"Sure you are," Kent drawled, grabbing her ass before pressing a kiss to her mouth. "I'll go make some coffee," he said, then walked toward the kitchen.

When Kent was out of hearing distance, Braden grabbed my arm and pulled me into the living room. "Okay, how are you? How are your night terrors? Are you and Tripp getting along okay?"

"As good as can be expected, the same, and yes."

Braden frowned. "I need more info than that."

I sighed and sat down on her sofa. "I miss him. I miss him so much. But he's better without me. Even he knows he's better without me."

"How does he know he's better without you? Have you talked to him?"

"No. But he hasn't tried to find me. You said yourself he hasn't called you. He hasn't called Tripp. Nothing. I did what he wanted. Deep down he wanted this and he got it. So, I have to figure out how to live. That was my ultimate goal, anyway."

Braden pulled her legs underneath her as she sat down beside me. "You have a really hot biker dude helping you out," she said.

"I heard that," Kent called from the hallway.

Braden giggled and rolled her eyes. "Seriously. He seems nice. You aren't bonding with him? I mean, you're with him every day and night."

"I gave my soul to Woods. He'll always have it."

Braden sighed and nodded her head. "Yeah, I understand that."

"Glad I got *your* soul, Braden, because I'm not sure I can beat that biker dude's ass. He's thin but tall, and that type's always hiding muscles under his clothes that you don't see coming," Kent said as he walked into the room holding two mugs of coffee.

Braden laughed and I managed a smile. I could attest to Tripp's muscles. I spent my days with my chest pressed to his back and my arms wrapped around him. He had muscles all right. Lots of them. He also had tattoos, which had surprised me. I could see the wealthy, elite Rosemary in him at times, but he tried too hard to cover it with tats and swagger.

"Stop being jealous. Nothing is sexier than you in a suit and tie. That short blond hair and tanned skin. I know what I got and I'm not looking for another," Braden said as Kent bent down to kiss her and give her one of the mugs.

I didn't want to witness this kind of affection right now. At least with Tripp I knew it was cheap sex he was getting. The romance was a little too much.

Braden read my mind. She was good at that. "Go on and let us girls talk. We need time," she told him, giving him a look that I knew he'd understand. I didn't say anything. I needed him to go. No more touchy-feely.

"Sorry about that. I wasn't thinking," she said as he left the room.

"It's okay. I will have to learn to deal with that the rest of my life. Might as well get used to it now. Couples are everywhere."

Braden reached over and grabbed my hand. "You will find your happiness. I think you're wrong about Woods but I've told you that. He loves you. I know he does. I remember the madman who came chasing after you just a few months ago. He adores you. I hate to see you let that go."

How could I keep it? "I couldn't stay. He was tired of my craziness. I heard him say it. He doesn't know I heard him, but I did. He was talking to Jace about how hard it was to deal with me. He was tired of it."

"What! I don't believe that. You must've misunderstood him. I can't see Woods ever saying that. And let me tell you, if he did I will cut him. Cut. Him. You hear me?" She was already getting worked up. I should have kept that to myself. I knew that would send her into a blind rage.

"What did he say exactly?" she asked, setting her cup down and studying me for any sign of a lie.

"It was a conversation, really. I can't remember exactly."

"Bullshit. It is etched into that brain of yours and you know exactly what was said, word for word. Spill it."

She wouldn't give in until I told her.

"I was at the club and I was looking for Woods. I decided to take the stairs instead of the elevator, so I stepped into the stairwell and I heard him talking. I didn't want to eavesdrop but I heard Jace saying that he didn't know how Woods had dealt with the crazy as long as he had."

"And what did Woods do? Please tell me he shoved his fist up his nose."

I shook my head and let the numbness ease me. I couldn't think about what I was saying. "He said it was what he had to do. That he couldn't let me be alone but it was affecting his work." I stopped and swallowed, then looked down at my hands. Anywhere but at Braden. "He said that at least when Angelina was there, she helped." That part hurt the worst. Hearing him say that someone like her was easier. That she was what he needed. Not someone like me. The crazy one.

"Maybe he wasn't talking about you. Isn't his momma a loony bitch?"

"No. She's just mean," I explained. There was more. Jace had said more. "Jace said that Woods needed to get his ass away from the insane shit. He had a corporation to run. He then said . . . that Woods dropping what he was doing to deal with my batshit crazy episodes wasn't fair. That he needed to fix the problem."

"Woods better have beat his ass then," Braden said, her face turning red.

I should've changed the subject so I could calm her down. But I needed her to understand that I had left Woods for him. This was what he wanted. He just didn't know how to ask for it. "Woods said he couldn't. Then he asked how he would do that."

Braden shook her head, her eyes wide with disbelief. "That just doesn't sound right. That isn't the same man I talked to . . . that I talked to back when he came to get you a few months ago."

"No. It's the man who had the responsibility of a country club and his mother laid on his shoulders overnight. He has real problems and concerns. I'm more than he can handle now."

Braden kept shaking her head. It would take her a while to process all of this. I hadn't told Tripp about that conversation.

I hadn't wanted to talk about it. He hadn't pressed me the way Braden had, either.

"You're not crazy. You're not insane."

"I know you believe that. But it's in my blood, Braden."

She gave me a sad smile. "No. It's not. There's something I need to show you and a lot I need to tell you. While you've been riding on the back of a hot stud's bike for two weeks, I've been doing some research."

"What? What do you mean 'research'? On what?"

"Della Sloane, you were adopted."

Woods

Darla Lowry, my golf course manager, was now a board member. She was the one thing my dad had gotten right. I trusted Darla with my life. With Jace planning on marrying Bethy, Darla's niece, we were just tying the family knot tighter. Darla was also wise. She was older than me and she had seen this club grow and flourish for over twenty-five years. She deserved a seat on the board. She also deserved the paycheck that came with that seat.

My phone rang and I glanced down to see Braden's number. I hadn't talked to her in a few days but she always called when she had any information on Della.

"Hey," I said, praying this wasn't going to be something bad.

"I know why she left. There was more to it, just like I said there was. But before I tell you anything I need you to make me a few promises and listen to all I have to say, because I'm not scared of you or your money, Woods Kerrington. I will hunt you down like a dog and bury you. Do you understand me?" Braden was fired up and ready to attack.

"If you can help me get Della back I will walk on fucking water," I replied.

"Good. I thought so. However, she thinks very differently.

113

She's of the belief that she has done you a favor. That you wanted to get rid of her and didn't know how. That she walked away and now you're relieved and living the good life."

"What? Why the hell? What the fuck gave her that idea? Did Tripp tell her that? Because I swear to God I'll kill him."

"Sit down and take a breath. You did this. Don't go pointing fingers at other people. First, I have to tell you about a conversation Della overheard the day before she ran off. You had better tell me what she really heard, because what she thinks she heard will get your ass killed, and sexy biker dude will get off scot-free. *Capisce?*"

"Please tell me what she heard, because I honestly have no idea."

"Did you have a conversation in the stairwell with your friend Jace that day?"

The stairwell? I sat down in my chair and thought back to before Della ripped my world away. I had talked to Jace that day. About my mom. "Yeah, I did."

"And . . ."

I wasn't sure what she wanted me to say. "And what?"

Braden let out a loud sigh. "What did you and Jace talk about?"

Hell, I couldn't remember. My mother was stressing me out. I was planning on installing the new board. I was going to let Della come back to work and stop smothering her. Nothing that should've upset her. "I can't think of one thing I said that would have made her leave me."

"So Jace never told you that you had to stop dealing with her crazy ass? And you didn't say that it was affecting your work and it was easier to work with Angelina? And Jace didn't say that you had to get rid of the batshit crazy because you had a corporation to run?"

I shot up out of my chair. "What?" I roared.

"I didn't think so. Didn't sound like you at all. If someone had called Della batshit crazy you would have beat their ass. Della, however, felt sorry for you for having to put up with her and thought it was in your best interest if she left."

"Holy hell! I swear to God I never said that. Jace never said that. I would've killed him. We were talking about . . . we were talking . . . oh, motherfucker." I knew what she'd heard. She hadn't heard everything. She'd just heard enough.

"Please tell me you didn't just have an epiphany and this conversation did actually happen," Braden said, warning me.

"No. Of course not. I mean, it did but we weren't talking about Della. God! Never Della. We were talking about my mother. She had just caused problems for me at the club and I was talking to Jace about how to deal with her. I . . . fuck! I can't believe she thought we were talking about her. I'm coming to get her. I can't do this anymore. I have to explain this to her. She has to know."

"*No!* Shut it, Kerrington. I told you at the beginning of this conversation that you would do just as I said. I'm not done talking to you and telling you everything you need to hear. So calm down and put your damn keys away. When it's time for you to come get her, I'll let you know, but this time I think it's real important that she come back to Rosemary on her own. She ran. She needs to find her way back. The cavalry can stay put and be patient."

"I have to see her, Braden!"

"Would you shut up and listen to me? I have information

for Della that she needs to deal with first. She thinks she's going to be mentally ill because her mother and grandmother were. She thinks that staying with you means you can't have kids because their mother could snap at any time and go insane. She loves you more than she loves herself. So she's making sure you don't suffer that ridiculous fate she's convinced you'll have with her."

"We won't have kids. I just want her. If she's scared of that, fine. We won't have kids. I have to tell her I just want her."

"Yeah, yeah, yeah, I know you do. Shut up, I'm not done," Braden snapped into the phone. I fisted my hand around my truck keys and moved to stare down at my truck parked outside. I could get to her in five hours.

"Della was adopted."

So many emotions ran through me at once, I wasn't sure if I was going to weep or cheer or fall to my knees and take deep, even breaths. Holy fuck. This was a game changer.

"She was adopted?" I managed to choke out.

"Yep. She was adopted. Her adoptive parents were scared to have kids because they were afraid that Della's grandmother's mental illness was genetic. So they adopted a boy from the foster system. He was two when they adopted him. Then a couple years later they adopted a baby girl from a teenager who wasn't ready to be a mother yet. You know the rest."

She was adopted. Her fear of being mentally ill like her mother was unfounded. "Does she know?"

"I told her today. She knows. I've set up a meeting with her birth mother. She's a kindergarten teacher. She's married and has a ten-year-old son and an eight-year-old daughter. They live in Bowling Green, Kentucky. Her name is Glenda Morgan and she wants to meet Della. She said she tried looking for her after her son was born. She realized what she had given up and she wanted to make sure she was okay. But the file was closed and it cost money she didn't have to get an investigator. Her husband had agreed that with their income tax refund this year they would find her daughter instead of taking a family vacation. So when the investigator I hired found her she was as thrilled as I was."

I wanted to like this woman, but knowing that her decision to give Della up had been the reason for the hell Della had lived through made it hard for me to forgive her. Where was the guy who knocked her up? Did he not care he'd given up a child?

"What about her birth father?" I asked.

"Glenda has contacted him. His name is Nile Andrews. He lives in Phoenix, Arizona. He's a dentist. Also married, with triplets. All girls. He wants to meet Della, too. His wife is being supportive of his decision."

A kindergarten teacher and a dentist.

"I've seen a photo of her birth mother. She looks like her."

"Please let me come. I want to be with her through this. She needs me."

"No, Woods. What she needs is to feel like she's strong. Like she can handle all of this on her own. She knows she's not going insane now. That's big. Real big. She's lived with that fear for so long. It's crippled her. She has to find her own strength now. And she needs to come back to you on her own. With the belief that she is strong and worthy of you."

"Worthy of me? What the fuck does that mean? I belong to her. How can she not be worthy of me?"

"I know this and you know this but she has to figure this out on her own. She had shit for a life. I held her hand for years. Then she left me and within months she had you holding her hand. No one can hold her hand this time."

"I don't want her to be alone."

"This isn't about what you want, Woods. It's about what Della needs."

I pressed my forehead against the window and closed my eyes. I didn't want her to be right. I didn't want to wait for Della. But this wasn't about my wants. Della loved me more than herself. She loved me enough to walk away because she thought it was best for me. It was time I proved I loved her more than I loved myself.

"Okay. But please, keep me updated."

Braden let out a relieved sigh. "I knew you'd do the right thing. Just so you know, I think you're worthy of her, and that's a high bar to reach. You promised to walk on water and I happen to believe Della already does."

Della

Her name was Glenda. When she'd given birth to me it had been Glenda James. She married when she was twenty-two. I would have been six years old that year. She married a man she met her freshman year of college. They had fallen instantly in love. They had kids. Two of them. Today I would be meeting her. And if all went well I would be meeting her family.

I was in a surreal moment. One I couldn't seem to snap out of. The mentally ill woman who raised me wasn't my biological mother. I wasn't going to become her. The woman who gave birth to me was a teacher. She was a mom and wife.

And my brother. He had been adopted, too. I didn't remember him but he'd been such a big part of my life. My mother had snapped after losing him and my father . . . or her husband. He wasn't my birth father and he had barely been my adoptive father before he was killed. There was so much my mother had told me that couldn't be true. She had said she was nursing me and led me to believe she had gotten depressed after my birth. But she hadn't been pregnant. She hadn't given birth to me. None of that was true. I didn't know what was true anymore.

"What are you thinking?" Braden asked as she drove down the busy streets of Atlanta. Glenda was driving down with her family to Atlanta. We were meeting at a coffee shop that Braden knew about. I wasn't sure I could eat a meal with this woman yet. I also wasn't sure what to ask or say to her. There was so much I wanted to know but then so much I didn't.

"She doesn't know about anything. I didn't tell her. I found her but I didn't feel like it was my story to share."

I wasn't sure I would be telling her about my life either. "What if I don't know what to say once I see her?"

"Then don't say anything. Do what you feel comfortable with. If today all you're ready for is 'hello,' then that's what we will do. When you want more we'll make arrangements to meet with her again."

Braden always made everything sound so easy. This woman had put her family in a car and had driven down to Atlanta to meet me. I had to say more than *hello*. "You won't go in with me?" I asked again. Braden had informed me that I had to do this on my own. It was my chance to prove to myself I was strong. That I was brave and that I didn't need someone to hold my hand. Though right now I was thinking I needed someone to hold my hand. I was terrified.

"Don't do this to me. I want to go with you. I hate the idea of you going by yourself, but this is for you, Della. This is for you."

She was right. Braden was always right. I nodded. "I know. Thank you."

I watched as she pulled the car into a parking spot in front of a quaint little coffee shop. There were tables outside and inside. The crowd wasn't big and I recognized the woman who had given birth to me from the photo Braden had shown me, sitting at the table in the courtyard to the left of the building. She had a cup of coffee in her hand and she was twirling it around nervously. This was scary for her, too, I guess. But she was brave. She was here alone.

"There she is," Braden said, pointing toward Glenda.

"I see her," I replied, and reached for the door handle.

"You can do this."

I glanced back at Braden and smiled for the first time in weeks. "I know."

◇

Her eyes locked with mine the moment I stepped out of the car. I watched as she stood and looked at me. I made my way over to her table, still unsure as to what I would say to this woman. She had given me life but she was a stranger.

"Della," she said as if needing to check and make sure it was me. We had the same hair, nose, and mouth. But her eyes were brown.

"Yes," I replied.

She fidgeted with her hands a moment, then covered her mouth with one hand. "I'm sorry. I just . . . I don't know . . ." She dropped her hand and gave me a wobbly smile. "I've thought about this day. I've thought about it so many times and now I'm actually standing here, looking at you." She studied my face, taking in the features I already knew were hers. "You have Nile's eyes. He'll like that. He always loved his eyes," she said with a smile. "They're his best feature. I'm glad you got them."

I knew I should say something but I didn't know what. I decided that it didn't matter if she liked me or approved of me. I wasn't here to gain her admiration. I wasn't perfect. I was damaged but I was a survivor. I had that to be proud of.

"I like my eyes," I finally said.

She let out a soft laugh. "They're beautiful eyes. I was always jealous of Nile's eyes. I used to tell him they were too pretty to be wasted on a boy."

It sounded as if she still kept in touch with my birth father. I wanted to know about that, too. "Should we sit down?" I asked, pulling out a chair.

Glenda nodded and sat back down. Her coffee cup sat forgotten. "Your friend, Braden, she didn't tell me much about you. She said that you should be the one to decide what I got to hear. I want to know it all, at least everything you feel comfortable telling me. What do you do? Are you in college?" She stopped and smiled at me. "Sorry, I'll let you talk."

There was one thing I was sure of: Glenda wasn't going to push for my life story. It wasn't easy to tell, and I wasn't sure I wouldn't fade out while telling it to her. That was a part of me that I would keep to myself. If this woman remained in my life then maybe one day, but not today.

"I've been traveling around. I wanted to see and experience new things for a while. Then I plan on going back to college."

"That sounds like fun. Are you traveling alone?"

I thought of Tripp and realized I was going to have to send him on to South Carolina without me. I wasn't going there now. I had to decide what my next move would be. "I was traveling with a friend of mine. He's going back to his home in South Carolina this week. I'm not sure yet what I'll do next."

"That sounds exciting," she said, watching me carefully. I knew she wanted me to delve deeper into my life but she didn't deserve that.

I didn't say anything else. I had nothing else to say really. Now that I had seen her and I knew this was my mother, I felt like I was finished here.

· "I almost kept you. I wanted to. I loved Nile back then. He was the captain of the basketball team and everyone fell under his charm. But he'd picked me. I was his girl and I worshipped the ground he walked on. When I found out I was pregnant I wanted to keep my baby. I wanted to marry Nile and I wanted a family. But I was sixteen. I knew nothing of love and heartache. I didn't know what paying the bills was like or how much babies cost. My mother worked as a nurse back then and my father was a construction worker. They made a modest living and we lived from paycheck to paycheck. I, of course, didn't understand any of that. I was wrapped up in the romance of it all." She stopped and took a drink of her coffee. She was nervous telling me this but I realized I wanted to know why. Why had she given me up?

"Nile came from money. Lots of money. His mother's father was a congressman and his father was a surgeon. They had big plans for Nile. Being a teenage father wasn't on their list. I think he loved me back then. I really do. I've always thought he did. He told me he'd get some money and we would run away and raise our baby. We would get married when we turned eighteen. I was giddy with excitement. Until everything changed." There was a sadness in her eyes. As if remembering this was hard for her. It had been twenty years ago. I couldn't imagine she still regretted it. Especially with the life she had now.

"Nile was offered a full-ride basketball scholarship to the University of Arizona. He decided to take it. He told me he wasn't ready to be a dad and he didn't think I was ready to be a mom. We were too young. We had no idea what we were doing. I knew he was repeating his parents' words back to me. I was angry and hurt. He tried for a long time to talk to me and get me to forgive him but I was done with Nile. He had betrayed me. He had chosen a scholarship over me and our unborn child. As the months went by and my stomach grew bigger, he would go out of his way to help me at school and do things for me, like bringing me my lunch tray. I continued to ignore him. He wasn't standing by my decision to keep the baby. He wanted me to give it up." Tears filled her eyes and she gave me a sad smile before wiping them away.

"As the days drew closer to your delivery date, my dad lost his job. My mom had been forced to sign us up for food stamps just so we could eat. They were fighting all the time and I knew it was because they were scared. Soon there would be another mouth to feed. A baby who would need diapers and formula and child care if I was going to finish school. I didn't want that for you. I didn't want you to live the life I had been living. I wasn't ready to be a mom and I wanted you to have more. I loved your father. You were a product of that love. It took me until I held you for the first time to realize I couldn't do this to you. I couldn't take you home to the life I could give you. It wasn't enough." She paused and took a deep breath. "I kissed your fat little cheeks, then handed you to the nurse and told her I couldn't keep you. To find you a good home."

I sat there and stared at Glenda. Her story made sense. Sixteen-year-olds weren't ready to be parents. I felt sorry for her, and she had been young enough to believe that handing me over was a better option. Maybe if my adopted father and brother hadn't been killed, then it would have been. My mother may not have snapped mentally if they had lived.

"I'd like to meet your family," I finally said.

A grin broke across her face. "I would love that. Thank you, Della."

Woods

I walked over to the bar and took the glass of bourbon that Mitch, the club's bartender, pushed my way. It was after-hours and I was expecting someone. He'd texted me an hour ago.

Just as I lifted the glass to my lips, Grant walked in the door and scanned the room until he found me at the bar. He had been out of town more than usual this year. It was summertime. He should have been in his condo, living it up in Rosemary.

"Give me one of those, Mitch," Grant said as he approached the bar, and leaned against it before looking at me. "I'm back. What's up?"

"Where have you been?" I asked.

His mouth was in a firm, set line before he gave in and let out a sigh. "You don't want to know," he said, then took a long swig of the bourbon.

That meant he'd been with Nan. There was a story there I wasn't sure I wanted to know. Grant was Rush's best friend. They were like brothers. Rush's mom had been married to Grant's dad when they were kids. The marriage only lasted a few years but they bonded. What no one expected was for Grant and Nan, Rush's half sister, to do anything more than fight. They fought when they were kids and they fought now. Grant was a good guy. Nan was the world's second-biggest bitch. Angelina was the first.

"Nan," I said simply.

Grant took another swig and handed the glass back to Mitch. "Another," he replied.

"That's twenty-three-year-old Kentucky bourbon. It's meant to be sipped and enjoyed, not thrown back like a shot of cheap tequila," I pointed out.

"You're an elitist, Woods. Kiss my ass. I need more alcohol."

"Anyone who spends five minutes with Nan needs alcohol. The question is, why the hell do you do it?"

Grant threw back his second glass of bourbon and then looked over at me. "Not talking about her tonight. Why did you call me? What is going on?"

Good. I didn't really want to know about Nan anyway. If she came back to town, Rush was gonna be pissed. He loved his sister, but she hated his wife. So Nan had drawn a line and Rush had stayed on Blaire's side. Nan's coming back to Rosemary wouldn't be cool. I'd hoped she was staying in LA with her daddy. She'd recently found out the man she had grown up thinking was her father was not. Her real father was the lead singer of Slacker Demon. Apparently, Rush's momma liked sleeping with the band back in the day.

"I fired the board. I'm choosing my own. My father's board isn't for me. I want you on my new one."

Grant set down his glass and stared at me a minute. "What did you just say?"

"The club has a board of directors. The old one has been let go. Will you be on my new board?"

Grant motioned for Mitch to refill his glass. "Damn, I'm glad I'm back. Crazy shit happens here all the time. No place is as drama-ridden as Rosemary. Not even fucking LA."

"Does this mean yes, you will be on my board?" I asked, taking a sip of my bourbon.

Grant grinned over at me. "Hell yeah, I will."

I knew he would. That made four. I still needed to talk to a few more. "I have paperwork in my office for you to fill out. But tonight, let's drink. I need a distraction."

Grant pulled out a stool and sat down. "Where's Della?"

I had been expecting this question but hearing her name jolted me. She had met with her birth mother today. Braden was supposed to call me tonight and let me know how it went. I was anxious and needed to think about something else until I got that call.

"She left." I couldn't bring myself to explain anything else.

"She left? What the fuck did you do?"

"Screwed up. Missed some signs I should have noticed. Got too busy to see what she needed. Smothered her." There was a long list of things I had realized I was guilty of.

"Damn. Last I saw you two, you were worshipping at her altar. How the hell did it go south so fast?"

"It's not over. I'm waiting. She'll come back. I'm letting her decide if she can do this. In the meantime, I'm drinking a lot and living for phone calls from Tripp."

Grant put his glass down and let out a low whistle. "Ah, hell no. She left with Tripp?"

I just managed a nod.

"Shit, dude. I'm sorry. If you want my help kicking his playboy ass I got your back."

At one point that would have been exactly what I wanted,

but not now. Tripp was taking care of her. He was making sure she was safe. It was all I had. I shook my head. "No. It's okay. He's keeping me updated. He's making sure she has what she needs to be free."

Grant frowned and leaned toward me. "Am I understanding you right? Your woman is off with Tripp and you're okay with this?"

"She loves me."

Grant nodded. "Yeah, she does."

"She'll be back. This hand isn't over. It can't be. I went all in."

I didn't have to explain that to Grant. He got it. He smiled and leaned back with his drink in his hand. "You got this one, Ace."

My phone rang and I pulled it out to see my mother's name on the screen. I stuck it back in my pocket. I wasn't talking to her. I was sure she was aware that the old board members had been released. She wouldn't be happy about that.

"Is Nan coming back?" I asked.

Grant held the glass to his lips a moment longer than necessary. He was stalling. I knew that move. When he finally set it down he turned his head toward me. "Yeah. She's coming back. I'm heading over to Rush's when I leave here to tell him. He needs to be prepared."

"You ask her to come back?" I asked. Grant's attraction to Nan made no sense to me. He had seen how evil she could be. He had seen her at her worst. How could he want that?

"Hell no. But she's coming. Kiro bought her a nice, big, fancy house. The light blue one that sits over the hill on the south end of the beach."

Kiro was the lead singer of Slacker Demon and Nan's father. "Damn. I like that house. How'd she get that out of him?"

"He's trying to get rid of her. She hasn't been easy to deal with. She gives him hell every chance she gets and he's pretty desperate."

"Can't say I blame him." I would have done whatever I could to get away from her, too, if I was him. Nan was dangerous when she wanted to be.

"I feel bad for her, man. She knows he bought it for her to move her as far away from him as possible. She just wants his attention."

"He's the lead singer in the biggest, most legendary rock band of our time. He ignored her for most of her life. He isn't daddy material."

Grant frowned and I could see he was dealing with something. "He has another daughter. He treats her differently. He's affectionate with her. He loves her. It's obvious. But she's not like Nan. She doesn't demand things and she's quiet. I think that's what he wants. A meek, sweet daughter. Nan will never be that."

"Another daughter? Really?" I'd never heard of Kiro having a daughter.

"Yeah. She lives with him, too. She has what Nan wants and will never get. Because Nan can't be her. She can't be what Kiro wants. It sucks for her. She's always just wanted attention. Both her parents denied her that. Rush is all she ever had and now he has Blaire and Nate. She lost him, too. I can't help but feel bad for her." He took a drink and set it down, then stood up. "I get that no one understands why I have anything to do with her, and I'll be honest: at times, I don't know either. She's all kinds of fucked up and mean."

I nodded, because he was right about that.

Della

"*I* shouldn't have got you. If it hadn't been for you crying and keeping me up all night I wouldn't have been needing a nap. I wouldn't have let my little boy go to that store. It's all your fault, Della. All your fault. He knows it, too. He wanted to stay with me but I was so sleepy. So very sleepy. You wouldn't let me sleep." Mother roared and reared back and slapped me across the face. I stumbled backward and grabbed the edge of the bed before I fell down.

"If you had slept at night and let me be a good mommy to my little boy he would be alive. But you ruined everything. I didn't want another baby. Your father wanted a little girl. He said it would complete our family. You didn't complete us! You destroyed us!" I braced myself as Mother hit me again. I tried not to cry. I tried not to whimper. If I whimpered she would get angrier. I had to stay calm. I had to let her scream. She would cry soon and go to her room.

"Get on that bed and don't move. The monsters under it will get you. They will come get you for being such a bad girl. They know it's all your fault. They know what you did to me."

I never understood her when she blamed me for my brother's death—I was a baby when it happened—but I let her yell and hit me. If I fought back she only got angrier. Once she had hit me at breakfast and I didn't wake up until the middle of the night. I had been on the kitchen floor with a pillow under my head and a blanket over me. She had put two plates of food beside me.

I didn't fight back anymore. I was scared to.

"Get on that bed!" she screamed as I scrambled to do as she commanded. "Don't come out. I don't want to look at you," she said before walking away and slamming the door behind her. I heard the familiar click and I knew she'd locked me in. My door had always locked from the outside. She controlled it.

"Good night, Momma," I whispered as I pulled my knees up to my chin and rocked myself back and forth while I pretended that I had a better life. One where I could go outside and ride a bike.

◇

I opened my eyes and stared at the ceiling fan. I was in the guest bedroom at Braden's house. I hadn't woken up screaming. I had never dreamed of my mother and not woken up screaming with imaginary blood on my hands. Something had changed. The memory was one I'd forgotten but her words that day made sense now. I sat up and swung my legs over and stood up. I had dreamed and not screamed. I was afraid to hope, but I had never been able to do this. I opened my door and stepped out into the dark hallway. Braden would be asleep and I didn't want to wake her. But I needed to process this.

I walked to the kitchen to get a drink of water.

Braden was standing at the counter with a glass of milk, staring straight ahead in deep thought, when I walked into the room. Her eyes shifted to me. "Della? Are you okay? I didn't hear you."

I stood there as it really sank in. I had dreamed of her. Yet I hadn't had a night terror. "I dreamed about her. About my life then. And . . . and . . . I just woke up. No blood. I never saw the blood. I just woke up."

Braden stared at me as she processed what I had told her. Then she set her milk down on the bar and ran over to me. Her arms wrapped around me. "You're getting better. Already, you're getting better," she said in a teary voice.

I wanted to cry, too. I wanted to cry because I realized I might just have a chance at happiness. What if I was strong after all? What if, underneath all that fear, I had buried someone deep inside who was brave and could take on life without someone to lean on?

"I think I'm going to be okay," I said out loud, because I needed to hear myself say it.

Braden squeezed me tighter. "I know you're going to be okay. I know it."

We stood there holding each other in the kitchen for several moments before I pulled back. "I'm not going to go crazy. I won't snap one day and become her."

Braden wiped at the tears streaming down her face. "I know. I've always known that."

"But I didn't. I had seen her. I knew what she could be. I didn't want to be that, too."

"She was the woman who raised you but she wasn't your mother."

I nodded. I knew that now. I was going to be okay. "I want to meet my . . . I want to meet my birth father. I need to see him. I need to see his family, too."

Braden nodded. "Good. I think you should."

I stepped back and turned to go back to the bedroom.

"Della," Braden said.

I glanced back at her. "Yes?"

"Call him. He needs to hear from you."

She wasn't talking about my birth father. She was talking about Woods. I would have given anything to hear his voice. But I couldn't. He had moved on. He hadn't looked for me or tried to contact me. I had let him go and he'd walked away. I couldn't bother him now. "I can't."

"He misses you," she said.

"You don't know that. You assume it because you think what we had was a forever thing. But Woods has plans and I'm not in them. I gave him what he wanted. I'm not going to bother him again."

Braden let out a frustrated growl. "Della, a call from you wouldn't be a bother to him."

She loved me and didn't understand what I was trying to tell her. I knew better. "No, Braden. I'm letting him live. I'll find my way soon. First, I have to figure out my past."

She didn't say more as I walked back to the bedroom. I closed the door and waited a minute to make sure she wasn't following me before I let the tears fall. I didn't want her to see me cry. She would call him. She would try to fix this. There was nothing there to fix, but she didn't see it that way.

But now I knew I was going to heal. I was going to be okay. I had a future. I had to face what I'd lost. Losing Woods was my biggest mistake. I shouldn't have left him. I should have been stronger then and fought harder. But I hadn't. I would deal with that the rest of my life.

Woods

The ringing was in the distance. I heard it but I couldn't find it. Everything was dark. My eyes snapped open and the ringing started again. *Shit!* It was my phone. I sat up and grabbed it. It was after three in the morning and Braden was calling me. *Della. God, please let her be okay.*

"Is she okay?" I asked the moment I answered the phone.

"Yes and no."

"What does that mean?" I asked, standing up and looking for my jeans. If I needed to go to her that night I would.

"She had a dream about her mother. She didn't wake up screaming. She just woke up."

I stopped searching for my jeans. "What?"

"She had one of her dreams but she didn't have a night terror. She didn't get lost in her fears. She just woke up. She's already getting better."

"I'm coming there. I've had enough with waiting. I'm on my way. Tonight."

"No! You're not. You have to give her time. She's meeting with her birth father next. She met with her birth mother and then had dinner with her family all on her own. She needs to do all this alone. She's realizing she can do this. She's also finding out that she was crippled by her fears. She's overcoming that. Don't come here and confuse her. She has to come to you this time, Woods. She thinks you don't want her. She needs to face that fear on her own, too."

Fuck no! "You can't expect me to stay here and let her think I don't want her. That's not okay, Braden. It's not fucking okay. She shouldn't have to overcome a fear that's pointless. How can she think I don't love her? That she isn't my heart, my soul, my future? That's the one thing she should never doubt. That, she needs to know."

"Listen. I know this is hard and you've been great so far but give her just a couple more days. Please. She needs this. Remember this is about what she needs, not what you want."

I started to hit the wall again and stopped myself at the last minute. That wasn't going to help anything. I had to calm down. "When she left here she took my soul with her. I will always belong to her. I don't want her to ever think differently."

"Trust me, I know this. But she doesn't. She thinks you haven't tried to contact me or Tripp and you don't care that she's gone. That you're relieved she left. Before you run out to your truck, take a deep breath and remind yourself that you'll get to correct her belief in a few days. Just give her a few more days. She doesn't need you here messing with her emotions while she's facing her demons and figuring out that she's going to be okay. When she sees you again she needs to feel like she can be what you need."

"Two days. That's it. She comes to me in two days or I'm coming there. I can't do this anymore. It isn't for me that I want to come. It's because I can't let the woman I love believe I don't want her. I've done this for as long as I can stand it. Two days is all I'm promising," I told her.

"Fine, two days."

I dropped the phone to the bed and sat down beside it. Della had overcome her night terrors. She was getting better. She was going to be whole. If I could make it just two more days.

⬦

My mother had called and woken me up that morning. I told her I'd be at her house in an hour to talk. She was furious and I had been avoiding her calls. It was time I talked to her. She would know soon who the new board members were when I held a party at the club to celebrate their new positions. Everyone would know and she wasn't going to be happy about it. Dean Finlay might send her into a rage. She should be prepared.

When I arrived at her house, Harry, the chauffeur I'd hired for Mother after I fired Leo when I returned to Rosemary, was loading my mother's bags into her Benz. She was going somewhere, obviously. Good. That was probably best.

I nodded as I passed Harry. He was my employee. Leo had been my father's. Leo had also left Della in handcuffs for five hours in the back of a car and hadn't let her use the restroom. I'd fired him before I could get my hands on him.

"She's leaving, I see."

Harry nodded. "Yes, sir. I'm taking her to the airport at nine," he replied.

"Thanks, Harry."

I headed to the door and didn't knock. It was standing open. The house cleaner, Martha, was standing there, wringing her hands nervously. I was sure she'd seen and heard my mother's anger. I smiled at her reassuringly. Stopping at the bottom of the stairs, I called out, "Mother. I'm here."

Then I turned to look back at Martha. "It's okay. You can finish doing what you were doing. She won't kill me. Even if she's threatened to."

Martha didn't look too sure but she nodded and scurried off.

Mother came to the top of the stairs with her purse over her arm. "I'm leaving," she stated, as if I hadn't figured that out already.

"I see that," I replied.

She walked down the staircase and I waited for more of an explanation.

"You have chosen to defy your father's memory. You have taken everything he set into place and thrown it away. Those men you let go were a part of the Kerrington Club for over thirty years. They are trusted confidantes. You thumb your nose at that. You're a foolish child. I don't want to stay here and watch you destroy this legacy. Your grandfather was a silly man. He shouldn't have left anything to you. A twenty-five-year-old boy isn't old enough to run a business like this one. You know nothing."

I let her angry words seethe from her mouth. She needed to get this out and it was time I let her. When her furious gaze leveled on me and stayed there I decided it was my turn to speak.

"Those men were my *father's* confidantes. Not mine. I put in place those who are close to me. It's time for a change. The club will be run differently now. I'm not Father. But I strive every day to be like the man who built this club. I admire my grandfather and hope to be worthy of his legacy one day.

I hope you travel safely and will check in with me so that I know you're doing well. I love you, Mother. You may not believe me or even care, but I do. You're my mom. That will never change."

She opened her mouth, then snapped it closed again. I believed, deep down, that she loved me, too. But right now her pride was too big to accept that emotion where I was concerned. She pulled her purse up to her shoulder and looked at the door. "I'm going to our apartment in Manhattan. I have friends there, and I prefer to live there now. Rosemary has changed."

Yes, it had. And I hoped it would keep changing. "I wish you happiness," I replied.

She didn't look back at me. I watched as she walked out the front door with the click of her heels echoing through the house. She would come back one day. She would love me one day. But for now, she had to go. She had to be mad. And letting her go was something I could do.

Della

Nile Andrews had my eyes. Or I had his. When his eyes met mine as I stepped into the restaurant, I could see that he noticed it, too.

I was more nervous about this than meeting Glenda. I'd never had a father. I didn't know what that felt like. What a meeting with the man whose sperm gave me life would even be like. My first question had been, did he really want to have this meeting? The answer was clearly yes. He'd boarded a plane to Atlanta hours after I'd called him that morning. He said he could meet me at seven at this restaurant. I had been surprised by his desire to come here so soon. I had even expected him to make excuses.

"Hello, Della," he said as he stood up and held out his hand for me to shake.

"Hello, Nile," I replied, slipping my hand into his. He was tall. Glenda had said he played basketball and I could see why. His hair was a dark color that contrasted greatly with his blue eyes. He was a handsome man. I could see what Glenda's teenage heart had seen.

"I'm so glad you wanted to meet me. I've been waiting for that call since Glenda let me know she found you."

He hadn't wanted me. But he'd been a seventeen-year-old boy. I couldn't hold that against him. It wasn't like he had been an adult who had made the decision to give me away. He hadn't been old enough to be a parent yet. Not really.

"I like Glenda," I said simply.

Nile grinned and he sat down after I did. "Yeah, she's something else."

There was a tenderness in his eyes that surprised me. He had loved her once. It had been young love but he had loved her. It had been real. And somewhere deep down it had never really gone away for him. Glenda didn't get that soft look in her eyes when she talked about Nile. She admired the man he had become and said his wife was gorgeous and perfect for him. Nile reacted differently.

"I guess she told you about what happened," he said.

I nodded. "She did. I understand. You were both young."

He studied me a moment, then shook his head. "You look so much like her. It's amazing. But you got my eyes. My other girls don't have my eyes. They got their mother's. But you got them."

His other girls. He hadn't called them *his* girls. He hadn't made them sound exclusive. He had said *other*. Something in me warmed. In his mind I was one of his girls. I didn't know him. I hadn't even known about him until a few days ago. But he had always known I existed.

"Did you know that I was a girl . . . before you heard from Glenda?"

A frown creased his forehead, then a small smile touched his lips. "Yeah. She told me. After you were born she told me she held you. That you were perfect and that she'd given you away. I got drunk that night. Real drunk. Wrecked my dad's car and almost lost my scholarship. I went a little self-destructive for a while. I was a kid myself but I kept seeing this small baby whose face I had never seen, and I knew she was mine. But I'd never held her. I'd never been able to kiss her." He shook his head. "It was the hardest thing I'd ever experienced. Then Glenda moved. Without a word of explanation she was gone. I didn't see or hear from her for over thirteen years. Then one day she called me. She wanted to find you. I didn't want to. It wasn't because I didn't want to see you, because I did. I was just afraid to see her. She, uh . . ." He cleared his throat and tugged at his collar. "She's my one that got away. You never quite get over that one."

I felt like pointing out that she hadn't gotten away, that he'd sent her running, but I didn't. That ship had sailed. They were both married with kids. "What are your daughters like?" I asked. I had never had siblings. Not ones that I remembered. To know I had half siblings in this world was hard to comprehend. I was curious about them. I wanted to know if they were anything like me.

Glenda's daughter was young but she had a free spirit. She'd told me I looked like a princess. She asked me if I could fly a plane and told me that one day she was going to fly planes. I had been fascinated with her. All her long blond hair, like her father's. Her name was Samantha but they called her Sammy. I liked knowing she was my sister. That what she was could have been me. I could have been like that as a child. I could have been so free. Knowing she would get a chance to live her dreams and have a family around her that loved her made me happy. It made the heaviness on my shoulders ease.

"Three of them are difficult but they're fun too. Jasmine is the oldest by one minute and fifty-six seconds, and she doesn't let the other two forget it. Jocelyn is the middle child and she's the most like me. She plans to be a basketball star. Then there is my baby, July. That's the month I met their mother. She's what warms me when I need it most. July is the perfect name for her. She's also the sweetest and most forgiving."

"They all have J names," I said, smiling at the idea.

"Their mother's name is Jillian."

I liked that. "I would like to meet them," I said.

Nile's smile grew. "I would love that. So would they. I told them about you after I got the call from Glenda. Jillian already knew about the baby . . . about you. So, she stood behind the idea of me meeting you. She would like to meet you, too."

"Okay," I replied.

The server appeared and we ordered our drinks and Nile asked if I wanted an appetizer. I wasn't really hungry at the moment so I told him no. Once the server left he turned his attention back to me. "What was your life like growing up, Della?"

This was a question that Glenda hadn't asked me. I had been prepared for her to ask me but she never did. Because of that, I had let my guard down with Nile. He was different. He wanted to know. He wasn't afraid to hear the answer. I could tell that Glenda was afraid of the truth.

"It wasn't easy. I wanted to meet you because I needed to know what the people who created me were like. I needed to know I was going to be okay. But I'm not ready to share my past with you. Honestly, I don't think you want details. If I were you, I wouldn't want to know."

Nile's face paled at my words and his jaw worked back and forth. I picked up my water and took a drink. I was more honest with him than I had planned on being. But the words had come out without a filter.

"You're wrong. I want to know," he said in a quiet tone.

I shook my head. "No, you think you do but you don't. And I don't like talking about it. I'm still working through some things. Meeting you and Glenda and seeing with my own eyes that you have healthy, happy children is what I need right now. It eases fears that I've lived with a long time."

Nile leaned his elbows on the table and studied me. "You're scaring the shit out of me," he said.

He had no idea.

"Nile, I want to get to know you. But I plan on taking that slow and doing it when I can deal with it. One day I'm sure I'll be ready to tell you about my life. Until that moment, I don't want to discuss it again."

He took a long, deep breath through his nose, then nodded. "Okay. Fine. But the father in me wants to fix things."

He wasn't my father. He was someone else's but he wasn't mine. He just provided the sperm that helped create me. "The male in you wants to fix things. Not the father in you."

He started to say something and stopped. A smile broke across his face and he leaned back. "Who is he? The man who wants to fix things for you?"

I fidgeted with the napkin in my lap. "I'm not talking about that, either."

"Why not? Did he hurt you?"

I shook my head. "No, he never hurt me."

Woods

I stood looking out the window of the conference room while I waited on my new board members to arrive. I had now talked to all of them. Everyone I had asked had agreed. Well, everyone except one of them. He would come around though. In time.

My thoughts went back to Della. I had twenty-four more hours before I was going after her. She would arrive here by then or I was going to Georgia and Braden could get over it. I had agreed with her at first but I didn't agree now. It was taking too long. Every day Della was away from me, she convinced herself even more that I didn't want her.

"I feel like a badass," Jace drawled.

I turned to look at him. He was standing in the doorway with a cup of coffee and a grin on his face. "When did we get so damn old?" he asked, then chuckled and walked inside.

"We're not old," I replied.

"Who's old? I'm not fucking old," Thad said as he followed Jace into the room.

I had debated asking Thad to be a part of the board. He was rarely serious and he still thought he was seventeen most of the time. But he was one of us. His father had been a board member. He should be one too.

"I'm old. That's who's old," Darla announced as she walked into the room with her iPad in her hands, typing away at it. She was always working. That was why she was the best.

"No, you're not. You're wise," I assured her.

She snorted and barely glanced up from what she was working on before she took her seat.

"This kind of feels like the knights of the fucking round table," Grant said as he sauntered into the room with a grin and a glass of what I assumed was bourbon. He really was drinking a lot more these days. I wondered if Rush knew about this.

"This needs to be quick. Nate's checkup is in two hours. I have to be there. They weigh him and shit. I don't want to miss that," Rush said as he walked into the room, followed by Dean.

"I'm not missing it either," Dean said, reaching into his pocket and pulling out a pack of cigarettes.

"No smoking in here, Dean," I told him.

He grumbled. "You bunch of prejudiced asses. No one lets me smoke anywhere around here. It's fucking insane. I need to go back home where I can smoke a joint on that street if I get the urge."

I ignored his rock star hissy fit. We were all here. At least the ones who were in Rosemary. We were missing two. One would take her place soon. The other still had his shit to figure out.

"Are you drinking bourbon this early?" Rush asked, looking at Grant with a frown.

Grant rolled his eyes and leaned back, propping his feet on the table. "Yeah," was his response.

"Really? You've started drinking whiskey before lunch?" Rush wasn't giving in and I really didn't want them having this fight in here.

"He's fucking your sister. Hell, anyone that stupid has to drink to stay sane," Dean said in a bored tone.

Shit. This was gonna go downhill fast.

"Don't respond to that, either of you," I said, standing at the head of the table.

"It's okay. It's true," Grant said, and held up his drink with a grin that didn't reach his eyes.

Rush swore under his breath.

"Harlow's too damn sweet for you. You know that, don't you, boy? She don't need Nan's seconds. She's too good for that. She's the kind of girl you can look at but can't touch. They're too unattainable for guys like us. Only those who can reach the pedestal she's on can touch her," Dean said.

"Harlow?" Rush asked, looking at his dad in confusion. "What's Harlow got to do with this?"

Dean just grinned. "What happens in LA stays in LA." He winked at Grant. "Don't it, boy?"

Yeah . . . there was a lot I didn't know. I was pretty damn sure I didn't want to know either. "Okay, let's get off Grant's private life and let's focus on the point of this meeting. As you all know, you are now my board of directors. I don't make decisions without meeting with this group and discussing it. You are my advisers. It's time to take the Kerrington Club into the next generation. We're going to do that together."

Darla's pleased smile as she sat back and listened to me talk meant more than she could have known. She was proud of me. Right now, I needed someone to be proud of me.

"Does this mean we can get rid of those damn coming-out balls? That shit is ancient," Jace said.

"Hey. Don't knock the coming-out ball. The girls get all sentimental, which leads to horniness," Thad argued.

"Could you please watch what you say in here, Thad? We have a lady on the board and another will be joining us soon."

Thad looked properly guilty. "Sorry, Miss Darla," he said sheepishly.

"No worries, Thad. I've been watching your horny ass screw through my cart girls for years."

The entire room went silent, then burst into laughter. This was a good group. We would make my grandfather proud.

Della

I opened the door as Tripp came walking up to it. I'd been expecting him. I had called him over an hour ago. Told him we needed to talk.

"You look good, Della. Much better than the girl I left here," he said before stepping into the house.

"Thank you. A lot has changed," I said, then motioned for him to go to the living room.

"Apparently it is a good change. You look almost happy."

Almost was a stretch. I wasn't happy. I missed Woods. I missed him so much it hurt. "Not sure if I'll be able to achieve happy, but I hope to," I said simply.

Tripp sat down in the closest chair, stretched his legs out in front of him, and looked up at me. "Talk, Della girl. I'm listening."

"I'm not going to South Carolina. I'm not sure what I'm going to do next but I won't be going with you. Thank you for everything. Thank you for putting up with me for the past two weeks and helping me when I needed it. What you did means more than words could ever express. I promise to pay you back every penny you spent. As soon as I get a job I'll start sending you money. I have your address."

Tripp frowned. "Don't send me any money. Keep it. I had fun. I had a traveling buddy for a while."

I wasn't going to let him get away with that. I had taken two weeks of his life on the road and now he was staying in Atlanta this week while he waited on me. "No. I'm paying you back."

Tripp smirked and shook his head. "I won't argue with you right now," he said.

"I found out some things this week," I told him. "I'm not having night terrors anymore. I still have dreams and there're still bad memories but I don't get scared. The fear is gone. I just wake up."

Tripp's eyes went wide and he beamed at me. "That's awesome, Della."

I nodded because I agreed. It was amazing. I had conquered something. "Yeah, it is."

"Are you going back to Rosemary?"

I wasn't sure. Every minute that passed in which I didn't have a panic attack and have to fight off the fear that used to overwhelm me, I wanted to go back. I wanted to show Woods that I was complete. I wasn't broken anymore. I was whole. He could love me. I was safe to love. But had I burned that bridge?

"I don't know," I replied.

Tripp bit his bottom lip. He did that when he was thinking. Finally, he let it pop free. "Listen. I can't say much because it isn't my place, but go back. If you want to go back. Be brave and go back."

I wish it was that easy. "What if he doesn't want me back?"

Tripp shook his head. "Not possible. Trust me."

"I left him. All I left was a note. He hasn't looked for me. He must hate me."

Tripp stood up and paced back and forth in front of the fireplace while biting his bottom lip again. What was he so worked up about?

I watched him, waiting for him to say something.

Finally, he stopped and ran his hand through his hair, pulling on the ends a little, like he was having a hard time with something. "Tripp, what's wrong?" I asked.

He stared at me hard a minute. He knew something. *Is Woods dating someone else already? Surely not. Oh, God. I'm going to be sick. Could he move on like that?*

"The money, it was all—"

"All because he was a good friend and wanted to help you, Della. Wasn't it, Tripp?" Braden's voice startled me as she interrupted Tripp.

He swallowed hard, then nodded. "Yeah," he finally said.

That wasn't what he was going to say. Braden knew what he was going to say and she had stopped him. She was keeping something from me. What was it?

I stood up and spun around to look at her. "Is he with someone else?" I asked. Just saying it ripped me into pieces. If she said yes I would crumple to the floor. I wouldn't be able to deal with that.

Her eyes were determined. I could see she wanted to tell me but she wasn't going to. "I think you need to go back to Rosemary and take back your man, if that's what you want. I think that if you love Woods Kerrington, then you need to be brave enough to put your heart on the line and go after him. You need to stop fearing things, Della. This is your last obstacle. Face it." Her voice cracked. "Please, Della. Go get him. If you want him. Go get him."

He had moved on. I sank back down on the couch. "Oh, God," I gasped as the pain started filling every inch of my body.

"No, Della—"

"Shut up, Tripp," Braden snapped. She wanted me to know the truth. Tripp was trying to ease my pain because he was a good guy but Braden loved me enough to be honest.

"How do I go after him? He doesn't want me," I said, my voice no more than a whisper.

Braden knelt down in front of me. "You are beautiful, smart, kind, and selfless, and you're the best friend I've ever had. I love you like a sister. You are my family. I've watched you hurt and I've watched you hide from your fears as if they really were those monsters under your bed that your mother threatened you with. In two days I've seen you face life with a strength I knew was in there but I'd never seen you use. If you want Woods Kerrington—if he is your forever—then go get him. Don't doubt yourself. Don't doubt your importance. People don't love you and forget you, Della. You're unforgettable."

I covered my mouth to smother a sob. Braden didn't reach for me and hug me. She didn't offer words of comfort. She just knelt there and watched me. She was waiting on me to decide. She was betting on me. When the rest of the world thought I was hopeless, she bet on me. She believed in me.

So had Woods.

"Can I have one last ride?" I asked Tripp as I raised my gaze to meet his.

"You know it," he replied.

Braden let out a loud sob as she stood up and wrapped her

arms around me. "I'm so proud of you. You did it, Della. You did it," she said into my hair as she cried in my arms.

I smiled over her shoulder at Tripp, who was getting a little teary-eyed himself.

He gave me a thumbs-up and winked, then he turned and walked out of the room.

Woods

I walked into my house and went for my suitcase. Della had four hours left to come back to me. I was packing. I was going after her. She wasn't going to come back. She was scared, and I'd be damned if I was going to continue to let her think I didn't want her. Whatever reasons Braden had could go to hell. I was going to get my woman. I was going to make sure she damn well knew I loved her with all my heart.

My phone rang and I froze. *It could be her. She could be coming back.* I was almost scared to hope. I reached into my pocket and pulled out my phone. It was Tripp.

"Yeah," I said, then held my breath.

"Get your ass ready. She's coming back."

I sucked air into my lungs and threw my head back as my heart started beating again for the first time since she'd walked away from me. Della was coming back.

"Are you sure?" I asked.

"She's packing her bag and telling Braden good-bye. I ain't gonna lie, dude. That was a tough scene in there. I was real damn close to telling her the truth and sending her back to you, but Braden is hard-core. She was determined that Della make this decision. When she broke and agreed to come back, even though she thinks you've moved on, it was emotional."

"What are you talking about? Why does she think I've moved on? What the hell does that mean?" Had Braden lied to her?

"She's convinced you're with someone else now. That the secret she can sense between me and Braden is that you've moved on to someone else. So, she's coming to Rosemary to win you back. She isn't just coming back to you—she's coming back thinking she has to fight for her man."

As much as I didn't want Della ever thinking I could even touch another woman, the idea of her coming to fight for me made me smile. "Are you bringing her?"

"Yep," he replied.

"Bring her to my house. Drop her off and leave. I'll be here," I told him.

Tripp chuckled. "Ah, damn, you mean I don't get to watch the make-up sex?"

"Careful," I warned him as my mind started making plans. I had a lot to do before she got here. "Go rent a car. Use the money I just put in your account. Don't put her on the back of your bike again."

"I'm a good driver," Tripp argued.

"Don't give a shit. If I have to think about her arms wrapped around you one more time I'll lose it. I don't want her on the back of your bike. Ever. Again."

Tripp let out a sigh. "Fine. I'll rent a damn car."

"Bring her back to me safe. And hurry."

"Yes, sir. Gotta go, here she comes," he said.

I hung up and looked around my living room. It was time

to start getting ready. She was coming back to me. I was going to make sure she never regretted it.

I dialed Jace's number. I needed Bethy's help.

"Hey."

"Bethy with you?" I asked as I began cleaning up the kitchen.

"Yeah, why?"

"I need her help. Give her the phone."

"Okaaay," he said. I heard him telling her it was me and that I needed her help.

"Hey, what's up?"

"Della is on her way back to me. I need rose petals. Where do I get a bunch of rose petals this late?"

Bethy squealed. "She's coming back! That's wonderful. I'm so happy for you!"

"Focus. I need rose petals," I told her as I put the last dish in the dishwasher and turned it on.

"I will get you rose petals. Don't worry about it. I'll be by in about an hour."

"Thanks," I told her before hanging up. I glanced over at the wall where the picture I'd smashed once hung.

I quickly dialed the next number on my list.

"Hey, Rob. I know it's late but the picture I brought you to frame—I need it. Now."

"It's not ready and I close in the next hour."

"A thousand dollars if you can get it to my place in two hours."

"Shit. Okay, yeah. I'll make it happen."

"Thanks."

Hanging up, I walked to the bedroom and started stripping the sheets. I hadn't changed them because they smelled like Della. My girl needed clean sheets. Once I had my room cleaned I dialed one more number.

"Boss?"

"Jimmy, I need your help. Close the dining room early. Tell everyone that there's a private member meeting or some shit. Just close it. I need the kitchen staff's help."

Della

"You didn't have to rent a car. I was fine with the bike," I told Tripp again when we pulled out of the car rental parking lot.

"Yeah, I did. Trust me," he replied with a smirk.

I was tired of arguing with him about it. He had been determined to rent the car and now it was too late to change his mind. I leaned back in the seat and stared out the window. I would be in Rosemary in five hours. I wasn't sure if I would go to Woods's house or if I would go to a hotel. Maybe I could call Bethy. There was always Tripp's condo. I could ask him for one last favor. I'd asked him for so many already.

"Are we going straight to Woods's place?" Tripp asked.

"Um . . . I don't know. Maybe I shouldn't blindside him. I could just go see him tomorrow while he's in his office. That way I won't have to just show up at his house in case . . ." I couldn't bring myself to say *in case he's with someone else.*

"What? You getting cold feet now? Can't do that. You want to get your man, then go get him."

"I'm not sure if that's the way I should do it."

Tripp shifted in his seat and cleared his throat. "Okay. Picture this: Woods is at his house with another woman. One he can't love like he loves you. You haven't been gone long enough for that. She's gonna get to sleep in his bed, where you belong, tonight. Unless you march up to his door and take back your man."

The idea of this faceless woman sleeping in Woods's bed and touching him made me physically ill. *No.* He was mine. She couldn't touch him. He was mine first.

"You're getting fired up, aren't you? Ready to take back what belongs to you? I think it's about damn time. Shame to let him sleep with her another night when he would rather be with you. She's just filler."

He was right. Woods wasn't in love with her. He had been in love with me. I could make him love me again. I could show him I wasn't weak. I was worthy of his love. I was going to fight for it. I would get him back—no one was sleeping over there tonight except for me. She was leaving. I'd make her leave.

"Take me to Woods," I told him.

Tripp let out a whoop and patted my leg. "Attagirl. You got this," he said.

I sure hoped I did. If not, I might've been on my way to making a complete fool out of myself.

⬦

When we were ten minutes away, I started having second thoughts.

"Maybe I should just go to your place tonight."

Tripp let out a short laugh. "Uh, yeah, no. Woods is already going to want to hurt me when he gets ahold of me. I'm not about to bring you back to Rosemary and take you to my place."

"But if he's with another girl . . ."

"Della, do I have to give you another pep talk? Because I will. You can do this. You came back here. You wanted Woods enough to come back and face this. It's time to face it, baby."

He was right. I knew he was, but I was scared of what seeing Woods with someone else would do to me. I'd come so far this week. I didn't want to turn into a whimpering lunatic in front of him. I wanted him to see the new and improved Della. Not the girl he had gotten rid of.

"He's gonna want to see you. I know you don't believe that but he will. I'm a guy. I know these things."

"He may want to see me, just not when he has another . . ." I couldn't say it.

"Remember, you aren't gonna let her have him tonight. You're back."

I nodded. Right. I was going to take back what was mine. Even if it wasn't mine anymore, I was gonna fight like hell.

"Okay. Hurry before I change my mind again."

"Two more minutes," Tripp said with a smile.

Those two minutes felt like hours. When Tripp finally pulled into Woods's driveway I almost wept with relief to see that his truck and my car were the only two vehicles there. That didn't mean he was alone, though. He could have brought someone there. The "she" in my mind still existed.

Tripp squeezed my hand. "Go get him," he said.

I couldn't talk. I was too nervous. I just nodded and opened the car door and stepped out. I hadn't even asked Tripp if he was staying and waiting on me or if he was going back to Macon to get his motorcycle. I couldn't think about that now.

I closed the door behind me and moved toward the stairs.

Then he drove away. I turned back to see Tripp pulling back onto the street. He stuck his hand out of the window and waved good-bye before speeding off. He'd just left me there.

I looked back to the front door and took a deep breath. Woods was in there. I was going to plead with him for a second chance if I had to. I was going to make sure I was the woman in his bed tonight.

The lights in the house were off. All I could see was a dim light in the bedroom. It almost looked like candlelight. *Please, God, don't let it be candlelight.* I gripped the railing as I walked up the stairs to the front door. He was never in bed this early. *Maybe he isn't here. Maybe he's with Jace.*

I reached the top step and stood there staring at his bedroom window. I was pretty sure that it was candlelight I was seeing there. It was flickering light. This was a bad idea.

No. .

It wasn't.

He was mine, and I'd be damned if I was going to let some other woman have him. I would shove the candle up her ass.

I closed the distance between me and the door and knocked several times, then stood back and waited. If it took a while, that meant he had to get his clothes on.

The door swung open and there he stood. He had on a pair of khaki shorts and a white button-down shirt. The sleeves were rolled up to his elbows. I loved it when he wore white. His dark skin was startling in white. I sucked in a deep, fast breath at the sight of him.

He didn't move. We just stood there, staring at each other.

It had been almost three weeks since I'd left. It felt like forever since I'd seen his face.

"Hi," I managed to croak out.

"Hi," he replied, still standing in the doorway, looking like a beautiful fallen angel. Whom had he gotten dressed up for? My nose caught a scent from inside and I stiffened. Someone was cooking. In the dark?

"Can I come in?" I asked.

He stepped back so I could enter the house. I didn't see her yet. But I smelled the food. *Maybe she isn't here yet.*

"Are you expecting someone?" I asked without looking back at him.

"Yes," he replied. His voice was low. He didn't want to tell me that. At least he was honest.

"Oh, I'll—" I stopped myself. I almost told him I'd be quick. I almost apologized. I wasn't going to do that. I was here to fight for him. Not lie down and let her have him.

"You should probably call her and tell her that your plans have changed," I said, turning around and facing him.

Something flashed in his eyes but the stupid lights were off and I couldn't see him well enough.

"Why's that, Della?" he asked as he took a step toward me.

I stood my ground. He was hurt. I had hurt him but I was back. Dammit. I was back. "Because if she steps foot in this house I will have to kick her ass." I snapped my mouth shut. I couldn't believe I'd said that.

A grin tugged at the corner of Woods's mouth as he took another step toward me. I didn't move away. I wanted him close. I wasn't going to run. "Hmm, someone's jealous," he said as he reached out and ran a finger along my jawline. I shivered.

"Very," I admitted. I wasn't ashamed of it. I was livid with jealousy.

"Why are you jealous, Della?" He took another step toward me, causing me to back up against the wall. His hands rested against the wall on either side of my head. "Who would you ever have to be jealous of?"

I was having a difficult time breathing normally. He smelled so good. The tanned skin of his throat was right there. I wanted to lick it. Taste him. "Anyone you touch," I said breathlessly.

"Then you only have one person to be jealous of," he replied, and lowered his head to nuzzle my neck. I trembled and reached up to touch his shoulders. I needed some support. There was someone else. He was admitting it. I wanted to hit him and scream and I wanted to grab his shirt and kiss him. Claim him.

"You left me, Della. You left me. You broke me," he whispered against my skin, and then ran the tip of his tongue up my neck and took a small nip at my ear.

"Who is she?" I asked, needing to remind myself that he'd been with someone else.

"Who is who?" he asked, pressing against me as he continued his assault on my neck as if it were a delicacy he craved.

"Who have you . . . who are you cooking for? Who's coming here? Who have you touched?" I asked, holding on tighter to his shoulders as my body went warm and weak.

"You. Always, you. Just you," he said, lowering his mouth to my collarbone.

What did he mean "me"? "I don't understand," I panted breathlessly as he ran his lips over my cleavage slowly and murmured about how good I smelled.

"What don't you understand, baby?" he asked as he moved his hand from the wall to cup my right breast.

I let out a strangled cry of pleasure. I wasn't going to be able to think clearly if he kept this up.

"You said there was someone else," I said as my body betrayed me and moved closer to him like a magnet.

"No, I didn't. You asked if I was expecting someone. I said yes. I was expecting you. You asked who I touched. I said only one person. You. Always you," he said, finally lifting his head to look at me. The heat I expected to see in his eyes wasn't what I saw. His heart was in his eyes. He loved me. It was right there for me to see. He was showing me with a look that he hadn't given up on us.

"You knew I was coming back," I said, wondering if it had been Braden or Tripp who had clued him in.

Woods cupped my chin gently in his hand and ran his thumb over my bottom lip. "I've known exactly what you were doing every day since the day you left me. I've made sure you had money to stay in hotels that were safe and food to eat. How do you think I kept from going crazy? I had daily calls to tell me how you were. Where you were. I stayed away because I wanted you to come back to me. I wanted you to want me. To want us."

He had been keeping tabs on me. He had cared. He hadn't just let me leave. Tears filled my eyes and I didn't care. I wanted to cry. I was happy. I was loved.

"Don't cry," he said as he began to kiss each tear from my face. "I can't stand it when you cry. Please, don't cry."

"You love me," I said, smiling.

Woods pulled back enough to look down at me. "Della.

That should have never been a question in your mind. You should have known that. If you didn't know that you had my soul, then I'm doing something wrong."

I reached up and grabbed his face and kissed him. With everything I had, I kissed him. I didn't have the words to make any of this right. So I showed him how I felt. How much he meant to me. His arms wrapped around me and he met each stroke of my tongue with his own. We stood there tasting and indulging in each other. It was perfect. I was home.

When I broke the kiss so I could catch my breath I reached for his shirt. I wanted that shirt off him. I wanted his clothes off. I wanted him inside me. "Now, I need you, now," I told him as I began unbuttoning his shirt.

"I have food. I was going to romance you first. Convince you to stay with me," he said as I pushed his shirt off his shoulders.

I caressed his chest. His broad shoulders always made me feel so small but safe. "I'm hungry and we'll eat but right now I need you inside me," I told him as my hands got busy with the buttons on his shorts.

"Then come to the bedroom," he said, his breathing as out of control as I felt.

"No. I can't wait." I reached for my sundress and jerked it over my head. I started to push down my panties and Woods let out a growl and took over. His hands covered mine and he pulled them down, and then he ran his hands over my bottom and pressed kisses to the insides of my thighs. "Get inside me," I begged. I wanted all the sweet kisses and I wanted to taste him, too, but right now I needed to be full of Woods.

"Fuck," he groaned, and stood up, turning me around to

face the wall. "You make me crazy, Della. I was gonna be romantic. You deserve romantic."

"I want you to fuck me hard. Fill me up and remind me that I'm yours," I begged.

Woods's body shuddered behind me just before he grabbed my hips and entered me with a yell.

"God, yes! So tight. So hot. This is mine," he said as he stopped and caressed my butt, then slapped it hard one time. "Mine. All this is mine."

"Yes, it's yours," I told him, and pressed back against him.

He let out another animalistic grunt and began moving in and out of me. With each thrust I climbed closer to the release I knew would fill me with completion.

"No one touches my pussy. This is my pussy, Della," he said in a growl before slipping his hand around me and running his fingers over my clit.

I went off like a rocket from his touch. "Yes! That's it, baby, come on my dick. That's my girl." His words made me wilder. I bucked against him and begged him to keep fucking me.

My words caused his body to pause, then jerk again as he began chanting my name over and over. Each tremor through his body made me tingle.

"My Della," he whispered as he rested his head on my back. I moved so that he came out of me, then I turned around and pulled him into my arms.

"Always your Della," I told him.

He held me tighter and we stood there as our bodies hummed our pleasure and our hearts healed.

Woods

My welcome-home for Della hadn't gone off in the way I had planned. I hadn't meant to take her in the foyer against the damn wall like a madman. But she'd been saying things that made me lose it. She wanted to be fucked and my body wanted to give her what she was asking for.

That hadn't been the plan. But I'd needed it. I had needed to hear her say she was mine. The thought of Tripp riding that damn bike while sitting between her legs ate me alive. I hated it. I wanted to remind her who belonged between her legs. Only me.

The idea that she believed I could be with anyone else still blew my mind. If she didn't know how completely I loved her, then that was my fault. I had failed her. I would fix that.

After I dressed her I brought her into the dining room. Jimmy had brought the staff over and set up a table complete with a linen tablecloth, candlelight, and roses. He had also brought the meal. It was Della's favorite special that we offered at the club. I watched as she took in the room. I had an Erick Baker playlist playing low over the sound system. She shifted her gaze over to mine and smiled at me shyly.

"This is beautiful."

"You were coming home. I wanted it to be special." *I didn't mean to fuck you against the wall before you could even completely get in the house.* Although I didn't say it aloud, her blush made me think she knew what I was thinking.

She turned and then stopped. She had seen the picture. The one Bethy had taken of us at the beach one afternoon. We had been lost in each other and hadn't noticed that Bethy was taking our picture. I had been sitting on the sand and Della had been straddling me, facing me. Our gazes were locked, and even in the photograph you could see the way we felt. There was no question as to how much I adored her in that moment.

"You had it framed," Della said, staring at it. I walked over and turned the dimmer on the lights up so she could see it better.

"Yeah, I did."

"I love that picture," she said, glancing back at me.

"Me too."

She turned around and looked at me. "That girl in the photo was scared. Of her past and her future. She was scared to love you. That's not me. I'm not scared anymore. My past is what made me who I am. My future . . . as long as I get to spend it with you, then I can't wait to live it. I'm going to be okay, Woods. I'm not going to . . . snap. I have a lot to tell you."

I already knew but I wanted to hear her tell me. I wanted to know her thoughts. I knew she'd met with both her birth parents, and I wanted to hear all about that.

I walked over to her and reached out and took her hand. "I always knew you would be okay. I was with you. I would never leave you. I was here to be strong when you were weak."

"And I love you for that. But I want to be the strong one sometimes. I don't always want to be the weak one."

"I just want you. In whatever way I can have you. But I'm glad you're happy. I'm glad you feel strong. I want you to be happy with yourself. Because you make my life amazing."

She sniffled and then smiled. "We need to eat. I'm fighting the urge to force you to make love to me again or cry because that was so sweet."

I tugged her hand and brought her to my side. "Baby, if you want me inside you again you just crook your finger. This food can wait," I told her before pressing a kiss to her lips.

"I want you inside me again," she said.

I was at least getting her to my bedroom this time. I had plans in there.

I pulled her behind me to the bedroom and opened the door, then stood back and let her walk inside.

The room was filled with candles and the bed was covered in pink and red rose petals. Della gasped, then looked back at me and gave me a naughty grin. "I thought I was going to have to come in here and beat someone up because they were in your room. That's what I thought when I saw the candlelight in your bedroom window."

I chuckled and reached for her. "Mmm, as sexy as it sounds to see you go badass over me, I would never touch another woman. Much less bring one in here. This is our room."

Della leaned into me and sighed. "I think Braden and Tripp wanted me to think that you had another woman."

I smiled into her hair. "Yeah. I think they did, too."

"I'm going to kick their asses. I was all ready to kick someone's ass because of them. It's only fitting I kick theirs."

I laughed, then picked her up and carried her over to the bed and laid her down on the bed of roses.

She was beautiful. "Take off your dress," I told her. She sat up and pulled it off. We hadn't bothered to put her panties and bra back on in the hallway. She was naked and back where she belonged.

"Good girl. Now lie back and open your legs," I told her, and watched as she did exactly as I said.

My release from earlier was on her inner thighs. Her pussy was wet and swollen from the rough loving we'd just had. I pulled my shirt off and took off my shorts before kneeling on the bed between her legs. I ran a finger down her silky heat and watched her body tremble.

"My come is still leaking out of you," I said as I rubbed it over her clit.

Her breath stuttered and she bucked beneath my touch.

"It's so fucking hot to see my release on you like this."

I dipped my finger inside her, then ran it down her thighs. The possessive monster inside of me roared to life. "I want to mark you," I said as I slipped my finger back inside her to coat it with more of our mixed come, then rubbed it on the top of her mound.

"Oh God, Woods. Please," she begged, and moved against my hand.

"My come looks so good on you." I was fascinated with it. Seeing it soak into her soft skin. Knowing it was a part of me.

"Then please put some more in me," she pleaded this time.

I rose up over her and teased her entrance with the head of my cock. She cried out and tried to get closer. I slowly sank into her until I was completely inside.

"You're my all-in, Della. I'll throw it all away for you. I just want you. I'm all in, baby. This life with you, I'm planning on us."

She ran her legs up mine and smiled up at me. "This is it. This is our start. Take me home, Woods."

I dropped my head to her shoulder and began moving inside of her while our breathing hitched and we gradually climbed to the pleasure we knew awaited us. The place we could only reach with each other.

"Now, Della. Come with me," I ordered when I felt myself ready to explode.

Her immediate strangled cry as she began clawing at my back sent me flying off into nirvana.

Della

I opened my eyes and stared into Woods's eyes. He was already awake. The way he looked at me made me feel treasured. Like I was some precious jewel he wanted to protect. "Good morning," he said as his fingers continued to trace the length of my arm with a featherlike touch.

"Good morning," I said, smiling at him. "How long have you been awake?"

"You mean how long have I been staring at you?" he asked teasingly.

"Yes, that too," I replied.

"About an hour. I woke up and you were so damn gorgeous curled up against me I couldn't go back to sleep. I didn't want to sleep and waste time that I could spend looking at you."

My heart squeezed. "You have a way with words, Mr. Kerrington," I told him.

"You think?"

I nodded. "I know."

"Good, because I want to ask you about the past two weeks and I want you to tell me everything," he said.

"I thought you knew everything already," I replied, realiz-

ing it had to be Tripp he'd been talking to. Braden hadn't been
with me for most of those weeks.

"I know what Tripp and Braden told me. I want to know
everything that Della knows."

So they'd both been in on this. I couldn't be mad at them.
Not now. I was in Woods's arms. They had brought me back
here. They had made me face my fears.

"I almost didn't come back. I was scared to face you. I was
afraid you didn't want me. Braden and Tripp talked me into
coming back."

Woods smiled at me and reached over to tuck a strand of
my hair behind my ear. "Sweetheart, I was coming after you.
Your time was almost up. I had told Braden you had forty-
eight hours. I had started packing my bag when I got the call
from Tripp saying you'd be back in four hours. Don't get me
wrong. I'm glad you came home to me. But I wasn't going to
stand back any longer. I'd given you two weeks. I wanted you
back."

He had been coming to get me. That was why Braden was
so insistent that I come back to him. She wanted me to be
the one to come back. "I'm not sure what I did to score a best
friend like Braden, but I'm so thankful I have her."

Woods kissed the tip of my nose. "There were a few times
I considered locking her up long enough to get you and run."

Giggling, I moved closer to him. "But I came home."

"Yes, you did. And it was so damn sweet."

He wanted to know about all that had happened. I wanted
to tell him about everything. "Do you know I was adopted?"
He nodded. "Well, I met both of them. I even met Glenda's—
that's my birth mother—family. She has a daughter and a son.

Her husband was quiet but he seemed nice. I mostly watched her daughter. I wondered if I would have been so free and outspoken if I had lived her life. And I have my birth father's eyes. His name is Nile. He was the high school heartthrob. I can look at him twenty years later and tell that. He's handsome and I think he may still be a little in love with Glenda, which is weird. But I try not to think about it."

I continued to tell Woods all about meeting the people who gave me life. I hadn't told Braden much about each meeting and she hadn't pressed, but with Woods I wanted to tell him everything. I wanted him to know that Nile smoked cigars and Glenda used to sing. She wanted to be a country singer once.

By the time I had finished telling him about everything, he had sat up and leaned against the headboard and pulled me into his lap. He made small circles on the palm of my hand and stayed silent. So I talked more.

I told him about my fears and why I had left him. I told him that my night terrors were gone. I wasn't waking up screaming anymore. I was whole. I wanted to be a mother one day. I wanted so many things I'd been scared to want before.

He slipped his hand down over my stomach and I felt fluttery in my chest. "One day I want my baby tucked safely in here."

I covered his hands with mine. "Me too."

We sat there like that for a while and didn't talk. I had told him everything. Every feeling, every fear. He knew it all now. And he loved me. Through it all, he had loved me.

"Della," he said in a gruff voice.

"Yeah?"

"The idea of you on the back of Tripp's bike, with your

arms wrapped around him, and him sleeping in bed with you and holding you through your fears—it's gonna be hard for me to get over. I'm thankful he took care of you, but you're mine to take care of. I don't want to have to see his face for a while. I need time to get over it."

I moved so that I was facing him. "I never thought anything of those things. I don't have any feelings for Tripp at all. You were the only thing on my mind."

"I know. That's why he gets to live. But it doesn't take away the fact I'm a man and I'm possessive of one thing. You."

He could be so sweet and romantic at times and then so tough and male at others. I shifted to my knees and gave him a wicked grin. "Let me see if I can get that image out of your mind and give you a new one," I said as I kissed down his chest and moved his legs apart so I could get between them.

He was more than ready when I got down to the bottom of his flat, hard stomach. I grabbed his thick length in my hand and held it while I flicked my tongue across the head.

"Baby," Woods groaned, and bucked underneath me.

"Mmm," was my reply as I looked up at him while I slid him into my mouth until he touched the back of my throat, causing me to gag. He always liked it when I gagged.

Both his hands grabbed my head. "Ah, that's good, baby. So damn good. Take it deep. Oh, hell yeah, gag on it." His words came out thick and raspy.

I continued to work my mouth over his cock while he praised me. I wanted to give him a memory that I could send him back to every time he thought about me and Tripp. I wanted to remind him who I belonged to. He never needed to worry. My body was wired for him only.

"Come up here," he said as he caressed my head. "I'm gonna come in your mouth if you don't stop."

I wanted him in my mouth. I grabbed his legs and continued to take him as deep as my throat would allow me to while sucking hard on the tip.

Woods's hands got more frantic and he now had handfuls of my hair. Each gentle tug made my pussy clench. "Gonna come. Your hot little mouth wants it, doesn't it? My naughty baby wants it down her throat. Fuck, yeah. That's my mouth to fuck," he said before yelling my name and holding my head as he shot his release exactly where we both wanted it.

When he eased his hold on my head, I slowly slipped my mouth up his cock, then back down again, cleaning him. I licked the sides and then pulled his head back into my mouth.

"Motherfuckinghell, baby, you're gonna kill me. Stop," he groaned, pulling me up and away from his sensitive flesh. He held me against his chest as he caught his breath.

I traced small hearts around his nipples with my finger. "Woods," I said.

"Yes, sweetheart?"

"Next time you think about me with Tripp, remember that instead. Okay?"

His hold on me tightened, then he chuckled. "I'll do that."

"Good."

Woods

I'd had Jimmy bring breakfast, too, so all I had to do was get up and get it out of the fridge. While Della finished getting dressed after I'd feasted on her in the shower, I went and got everything ready.

I cleared the table from last night and toasted her Belgian waffle, then added the orange cream and shaved almonds to the top of it. I also put out a bowl of honey yogurt with figs and goat cheese. These were all items that Jimmy said Della ordered off the breakfast menu.

When she came walking out of the bedroom, her hair was pulled up in that sexy bun again and she was dressed for work. Good. I had to talk to her about the new board.

"I hope it's okay if I go to work today," she said as she walked into the room.

"Whatever you want to do," I told her, then pulled back her chair.

She took in the food on the table, then cut her eyes back at me and smirked. "You got Jimmy to help you with this."

I shrugged. No use in denying it. "I wanted to get it right."

She stopped and pressed a kiss to my lips. "You get everything right." Then she sat down at the table and let out a pleased sigh. "I'm starving."

"Wild, hot sex all night and morning will do that to you," I replied, and sat down across from her.

She blushed and reached over to take a fig. "Yes, I guess it will."

I was sticking with a Belgian waffle and butter. The fancy shit wasn't my thing. I took a bite and watched her eat some before taking a drink of my coffee and preparing myself to ask her to be on my board.

"I fired the board of directors. I hired a new one. People whose opinions I care about," I said, getting straight to the point.

Della put her fork down and stared at me. "Good for you. You're in charge; you need those close to you helping you with this."

I was glad she agreed. Not that I expected her not to. "I want you on the board, Della."

She had started to pick up her juice but she set it back down and looked at me like I'd just spoken a foreign language.

"What?" she asked.

"I want you on my board. I already have your paperwork ready. You just need to sign it."

Della shook her head. "I don't think that's a good idea. I mean, maybe later when you're sure, but right now . . . that's a hasty move. I mean, just three weeks ago you and Jace were worried about my, uh, problems being an issue. I can't be on your board. I'm better, but what if I relapse? You don't want that there and I know your friends agree. I heard Jace. He's gonna want to see that I'm better."

I had forgotten about that damn conversation she'd overheard. I stood up and moved around the table, then knelt down in front of her. "Della, I need you to listen to me. What you heard wasn't what you think it was. We weren't talking about you. Never you. We were talking about my mother. She had called board members and caused problems for me. We were discussing her because, unlike you, she really is crazy. Baby, I would never call you those things or allow anyone else to call you that."

I could see the relief in her eyes. She believed me. She hadn't brought it up all night and I'd been so damn happy to see her that I hadn't thought about it. But damn, she was here in my arms thinking I'd said those things. It was humbling.

"Oh," she said simply.

I smiled and stood up and kissed her. "Yeah. Oh."

"I should have asked you about it. I was . . . I didn't want to hear the truth. I was scared of it."

"Never be scared to hear the truth from me," I told her.

She nodded. "I'm sorry I didn't ask you about it."

"I'm sorry you thought we were talking about you."

She sat there and studied her hands a moment, then looked up at me. "I want to be on your board."

"Good. I can't do this without you."

She went back to eating and I had to force myself to eat, too, and not watch her. I just wanted to watch her do everything. Letting her out of my sight today was going to be hard.

⟡

I stepped off the elevator and Vince looked up to greet me. He started to speak and stopped. I watched him as he observed me.

"Miss Della is home, then," Vince said.

"Yes she is. How did you know?"

Vince let out a low laugh. "I'm old, Woods, not blind. It's all over your face, boy."

The grin that broke out across my face stayed while I went through my morning notes and made scheduled phone calls.

Right before lunch, Della stepped into my office with a sexy little smile on her face that was going to get her fucked up against my desk if she wasn't careful.

"I missed you," she said.

"I missed you more. Come here," I told her, holding out my hand for her to come to me. She walked over to my side of the desk and I pulled her down to my lap. "Have you had a good morning?"

"Yes. Have you?"

"It could have been better," I replied, slipping my hand up her skirt. She wiggled in my lap and slapped my hand away.

"Stop that. We have work to talk about," she said playfully, and then tried to stand up. I held her to my lap.

"Go ahead and wiggle, baby. It feels real good."

"You are so bad," she said, stopping me from slipping my hand between her thighs.

"I'm playing catch-up. I have three weeks' worth," I told her.

"Mr. Kerrington, Mr. Rush Finlay is here to see you," Vince announced over the intercom.

"Damn, Rush. Forgot he was coming by."

Della jumped up out of my lap and straightened her skirt.

"Send him in," I said as I watched her fix herself. I was going to mess it up as soon as Rush brought me the info on Nate's trust fund that he'd set up for Dean.

Rush walked into the room with Nate in his arms and a baby bag over his shoulder. That was funny shit. Rush Finlay, badass rock star's son, had a baby bag and a baby in his arms.

"Oh, you brought Nate!" Della's excitement interested me.

I watched her walk over to Rush and take Nate from him. She walked over to the sofa with him, cooing and making him laugh.

Rush's chuckle reminded me he was there. I shifted my attention back to him.

"She likes babies," Rush said with a smirk.

I hadn't known she liked babies. I liked watching her with Nate. Rush was going to be hard to concentrate on. "Yeah, she does."

"When did she come back? Or did you chase her down?"

"Last night. She came back to me," I told him.

"Told you that hand wasn't over," Rush said, then took a seat across from my desk. "Stop mentally fucking her while she's holding my kid."

I shot him an annoyed glare that just amused him. "Here's the paperwork for Nate's trust. Do the same with my paycheck from here."

"Done. I'll get the direct deposits set up today."

Rush let out a sigh. "I might just sit here a minute and take a break. Della looks like she's having fun and I'm beat. Grant was at my house late last night and we had to deal with some shit."

"Is Nan back?"

Rush let out a weary sigh and rubbed his forehead. "Yeah. She's back."

"Damn," I said, more for Rush's sake than anything.

"Yeah," Rush agreed.

Della

Nile was coming to Rosemary today with his family. They were staying in one of the condos on the club property. He had insisted on paying but Woods had gotten him to accept the free condo. I wasn't sure what he'd said but he had talked him into it.

I was excited about introducing Woods to him. I wanted to know what Woods thought about him. Deep down, I also wanted to show Woods that the blood in my veins came from normal people. I often forgot that myself.

"You look beautiful. Stop fidgeting. Nothing you do can make you any more beautiful than you are," Woods said as he reached over and took both my hands in his to keep me from pulling down the mirror and checking my face one more time.

"I know I'm being silly. I'm sorry. I just . . . I've not met Nile's family yet. His daughters . . . they're my sisters."

"And they're about to find out that they have the most beautiful, talented, sweet, brilliant older sister in the world. So stop it. Take a deep breath and know that you're amazing and they're lucky to get to sit in the same room with you."

Woods could say some of the sweetest things in the world.

"I really want to kiss you right now but it will mess us up."

He laughed and pulled the car into the valet parking line at the club. We were meeting Nile and his family there for dinner. "I'll get messed up any time you want to put those plump lips of yours on me."

"Save it for later, sexy," I said just as my door was opened by Bradley. I was glad to see he was still working out. I had hired him a month ago.

"Good evening, Miss Sloane. You're looking lovely," he said with a twinkle in his eyes.

"She's always lovely; hands off," Woods told him, taking my hand and tucking it in his arm.

"You scared that poor valet to death," I said, scolding him.

"Good."

I didn't argue. I followed him inside the club, trying not to smile like an idiot.

"Mr. Kerrington, right this way, sir. Your party has already arrived," Jimmy announced when we stepped into the dining room.

Jimmy shot me a wink before leading us over to the formal dining area reserved for special guests and parties. Woods had requested it so that we'd have privacy.

Nile stood up when we walked in. Woods squeezed my hand to reassure me.

"Hello, Nile," I said in greeting, then turned to Woods. "Woods, this is Nile Andrews. Nile, this is Woods Kerrington."

Woods and Nile shook hands and I heard Nile thanking him for the accommodations, which I had no doubt were extremely impressive, knowing Woods. I looked over at the three girls sitting at the table, studying me. Each one had a different expression. They ranged from nervous to curious.

"Della, I'd like you to meet, Jillian, my wife."

Jillian was tall and slender with long, dark red hair. Her skin was a creamy ivory color and her eyes were hazel. "It's so nice to meet you, Della. Nile has told me all about your visit. I'm anxious to talk to you myself, as are the girls." She had kind eyes. The high cheekbones and excellent bone structure made me think of an uppity elitist woman but Jillian was very nice and down-to-earth. She was what I would have expected Nile to be married to. I couldn't picture him with Glenda. They were nothing alike.

"I'm glad y'all could come visit," I said, glancing down at the girls again. All three of them had their mother's hair color and eyes.

"Della, this is Jasmine, Jocelyn, and July. Girls, this is your sister Della," Nile said, standing to my left. I hadn't expected him to call me their sister. That was surprising. I also wasn't sure how I felt about that yet.

"It's nice to meet the three of you," I said.

"I love your dress. Is it a Marc Jacobs? I swear, I saw one in the new Marc Jacobs line just like it."

"You have Daddy's eyes. I've always wanted Daddy's eyes."

"Do you live on this beach?"

All three of them began talking at once. I was a little overwhelmed but I liked that they wanted to talk to me. I started with Jasmine. "I have no idea who Marc Jacobs is. I bought this dress on a shopping spree with my best friend at a thrift store in Atlanta." I could see the fascination in her face at the idea that I'd shopped in a thrift store.

"I do have your dad's eyes. It was a pleasant surprise but yours are equally beautiful. You have your mother's fantastic hair." Jocelyn blushed prettily and I wondered if she was the shy one.

"And yes, I do live on this beach. It's a wonderful place to live," I told July.

"Do you always shop in thrift stores? I've always wondered what they were like inside."

"I can play the piano. Do you play the piano?"

"Do you know how to surf? I've always wanted to surf."

Again all three of them asked me a question at once.

"Girls, let Della sit down and breathe. You will have plenty of time to drill her with questions, but don't scare her away just yet," Jillian said before I could start answering their questions again.

Woods pulled out my chair and I took a seat. He then took the one next to me. I was seated across from Jillian and he had taken the seat across from Nile. July sat to my right. Jimmy came up and put my napkin in my lap.

"Sweet tea, Miss Sloane," he said as he set the glass down in front of me. I could see the impressed gleam in Nile's eyes as he watched Jimmy deliver our drinks and appetizers without our having ordered.

"Thank you, Jimmy," I said, smiling up at him.

He shot me a quick grin before leaving the room.

"He is swoony. I saw him when we came in and he winked at me," Jasmine said from across the table.

I bit back a smile. Jimmy was beautiful and he knew how to make women of all ages drool over him. And while they were checking him out, he was checking out their men. I'd caught him appreciating Woods's backside on more than one occasion.

"Jasmine, please," Nile said, frowning down at her.

"Sorry," she mumbled.

"July just kicked me. I was just asking her to pass the bread and she kicked me," Jocelyn said as she crossed her arms over her chest.

"All right, girls. That's enough," Jillian said, then looked over at me apologetically. "They were in the car all day and now they're overly excited about being here and meeting you."

"I'm fascinated. I've never been around little girls like this. Or sisters. It's very entertaining."

Jillian's laugh reminded me of tinkling bells. "You may not feel that way anymore before the meal is over."

Woods's hand slid over my leg and rested on my upper thigh. I had faced Nile the first time alone but it was nice to have Woods beside me now.

"I invited Nile to play a round tomorrow morning with me, if that's okay with you," Woods said, leaning closer to me as he spoke.

I liked the idea of his getting to know Nile. "Of course. That's fine," I assured him, and smiled over at Nile.

"Are you married?" one of the girls asked. I glanced back at them and saw Jocelyn elbow July.

"She's not wearing a ring. Don't ask that," Jocelyn hissed.

"No, we're not. But it's okay for her to ask," I replied, unable to keep from smiling at them. Their constant fighting made me wish I'd had a sister.

"Why not? You live with him, don't you?" July asked.

"July." Jillian was the one to scold her this time.

"It's okay, really. I want them to ask me questions," I assured her. Then I looked back at July. "I do live with him. He's my boyfriend."

"Mommy and Daddy lived together for two years before they got married," Jasmine announced from across the table.

I saw red splotches appear on Jillian's face but she just laughed and shook her head. "You need to stop listening to adult conversations. I swear, you know more than you're supposed to," Jillian said as she tried to cover her amusement.

"Does that mean you will be getting married, too?" July asked.

They really weren't going to let the marriage thing go.

"Maybe I will get married one day. I don't know that right now."

"Let's ask Della questions that don't pertain to her personal relationships. Okay, girls?" Nile said with a stern voice. I watched as all three nodded with a look of defeat.

"I have a boyfriend. Can we talk about him?" July asked.

"I would love to hear about him," I assured her. She beamed.

I heard Jasmine sigh from across the table. "Great, here we go," she muttered.

Woods

Della had opened up more than I expected to Nile and his family. Mostly it had just been to Nile's daughters. They had been drawn to her, too. Watching it had been heartbreaking and amazing all at the same time. Della could have had a normal life. Her father was a good man.

I had also watched Nile most of the night. He had watched Della and his girls, too. The pleased look on his face was hard to miss. He might never be someone that Della considered a father but I had hopes that she would form a relationship of some kind with him and his family. I thought she needed it.

"Tell me what you thought of Nile and his family," Della said as we walked into the house. She had been quiet on the ride back and I had left her alone with her thoughts. It was a lot to process without my trying to pull things out of her.

"I think he's a good man and he's a good father. The girls are well-adjusted and they are fascinated with you."

Della grinned as she slipped off her heels. "I liked the girls. Each one was so different. It was like they made this one complete person. I wonder what it must be like to know you have someone on your side all the time, knowing you can make snide comments and even push and shove but they'll love you when the rest of the world is against you."

I walked over and wrapped my arms around her from behind. "I'm always on your side. You can push and shove—hell, you can even slap me—but I will still be right here, ready to face the world with you."

Della leaned back against me and wrapped her arms around mine. "I know that. I meant growing up. Having a sibling to stand in your corner."

I understood what she meant and it broke my heart to think about the little girl who was so alone in dealing with a mother who wasn't there mentally. "You did find Braden."

"Braden found me. And you're right. She was always in my corner."

"I like knowing you have her. She loves you almost as much as I do."

Della laughed. "Don't let her hear you say that. She'll fight you for that title."

I wondered what Braden would do when I asked Della to marry me. Would she grill me? Make sure my intention was to treat her like a princess? I had no doubt I'd hear from her when the time came. I just wasn't sure about the right time.

I loved Della and I knew no one would ever take her place in my heart. She was the one. But marriage also meant a commitment that scared me. I'd been ready to ask her before she left me. Now I knew how quickly she could rip my world out from under me. Could I handle that kind of pain if she were my wife? It was making me even more vulnerable. I needed time to adjust to having her back. Having a Della who didn't wake up screaming and one I didn't worry about all the time.

"I love you," she said as we stood there together.

"I love you more," I replied. And I meant it. That was what kept me from asking her to marry me. That was my roadblock. I loved her more.

A knock on the door broke into my thoughts and Della stepped out of my arms to look back at me. "Who could that be?"

"Not sure. I'll get it."

◇

Jace was pacing back and forth on my front porch when I opened the door. His head snapped up when he saw me. He shook his head and went back to pacing. This was woman trouble. I looked back at Della, who stood watching me from the other end of the hallway.

"Looks like Jace needs to talk. We'll be out here if you need me," I told her.

A worried frown pinched her forehead but she nodded. "Okay."

I closed the door behind me and watched as Jace continued to pace.

"What's wrong with Bethy?" I asked. I knew that was the only thing that could get him to pace like a madman.

He stopped his constant moving and shoved his hands in his pockets. "She's . . . She wanted to get married. I mentioned it to her and she wanted to. But she's started to act different lately. So I dropped the marriage thing. I thought that was what made her go crazy. But she's just getting worse. Hell, what was I supposed to do? I can't get married if she's not ready. I sure as hell can't ask her. I don't know what I was thinking. Just because Rush and Blaire are playing house doesn't mean the rest of us are ready."

I was going to be here a while. I could tell by the frantic

tone in Jace's voice. I sat down in the swing. "So you've changed your mind on the marriage thing? Sounds like it scared Bethy anyway. Maybe you two need more time just being a couple."

Jace let out a hard laugh. "Yeah, I thought that, too. But she's just . . . reverted."

"Reverted?" I asked, trying to figure out what in the hell he was talking about.

"You know, reverted to the way she was before. She's drinking and wanting to go out partying all the time. She rarely sees Blaire anymore because she said it makes her sad. She wants what Blaire has but she says it's rare. We can't measure ourselves against that. But that makes no damn sense. I've been in two bar fights in the past week. Two fucking bar fights. Me. I don't fight, dammit. But she's forcing me to go save her drunk ass from men who want to touch her."

I thought about Della playing with Nate the other day and how sweet she was. But not once had she asked for the same thing. She never pressured me for more. I wasn't sure what I'd do if she did. I would probably give it to her.

"Do you want Bethy? Forever? Is she who you see yourself spending your life with?"

"I did. Before all this. I did. I thought we were ready. But now she's changed. She's acting like . . . she's acting like she did before. When all I wanted to do was fuck her because she was so damn good at it. I was addicted to sex with her. Then she stood up to me and drew a line in the sand and I came barreling through it because I realized, through all that sex, that I had started to care for her. I wanted more than just the sex."

Everyone knew this story already. No one had expected it. Jace was a trust fund baby and Bethy was a trailer park baby.

The two didn't seem to fit . . . until they did. "She could be drawing the line in the sand again. Forcing you to pick her."

Jace walked over and sat down on a padded bench and dropped his head into his hands. "If I thought that was it I would just propose. I would just ask her to marry me. Because, yeah, I love her. But I think she's hiding something. I don't know what. I try to overlook it but there are times—and they're rare—when she withdraws from me. I can't pinpoint when it happens. I can't figure out a reason—she just does. Then suddenly she's back the next day or a few days later, however long it takes, and she's my Bethy again. I just . . . she has to tell me everything. She has to explain to me what haunts her and why the hell she thinks going to a honky-tonk dressed like a cowboy's wet dream is okay. I'm tired of getting into fights with dudes bigger than me."

Della never did any of these things. I couldn't sympathize and now I was pretty damn sure he shouldn't propose because they had shit to figure out.

"You two need to talk," I said. I had no other words of wisdom.

Jace ran his hand through his hair and sighed. "I know we do. Every time I try and ask her about it, she starts drinking. The next thing I know, she's dancing on a bar somewhere. When she starts to sober up she tells me she wishes she was enough for me and that she wishes she was someone I could love forever. I tell her she is but she needs to tell me why she's doing this. Why she pulls away from me sometimes. She either starts crying or sucking my damn dick. Both get me completely distracted."

I had thought Jace and Bethy were fine. They were good.

They were always together. I hadn't imagined any problems with the two of them. Bethy was always so happy and bubbly. The Bethy he was describing wasn't someone I'd ever seen.

"I love her. I'm gonna do whatever the hell I need to to stop this. Because I can't lose her. I love her. She's the best thing that ever happened to me. All relationships before her pale in comparison. If she wants to get married, I'll propose. I wanted to wait but I don't think she'll ever tell me why she pulls away sometimes. Maybe if we're married she won't do that. If I put a ring on her finger then it will stop this drunken partying shit she's doing."

The only thing he'd said there that even came close to a reason as to why he should marry Bethy was the part where he said he loved her and she was the best thing that had ever happened to him. The other stuff wasn't good logic. "I think you need to get her to talk to you sober first. Lock her in a room and make her talk. Don't just propose because she's forcing your hand with this drinking shit. That isn't what marriage is supposed to be about. You gotta want this, man."

Jace glanced back at the door to my house. "What about Della? Do you want it with Della?"

Yeah, I wanted forever with her. "One day, but she isn't pressuring me. When the time is right."

Jace nodded. "Yeah, that's what I thought, too. But Bethy seems threatened by that idea." He stood up. "Thanks for listening. I needed to unload on someone. I couldn't go back to the condo and deal with Bethy after tonight. I just needed to talk."

"You're my best friend. I'm always here to talk when you need to. Besides, you kept me from losing it when Della left me."

Jace chuckled. "More like Rush did. I was scared to touch you. You were going apeshit."

"Rush was the only one strong enough to hold me back. But you listened to me and kept me sane while she was gone."

Jace nodded. "You're my family."

And he was mine.

Della

"*H*ush, *little baby, don't say a word, Momma's gonna buy you a mockingbird." Momma's voice rang out shrill and off-key as I stood outside her bedroom door and peeked inside. She was in a rocking chair in her room with the baby doll I wasn't allowed to touch wrapped tightly in a blanket. She sang to the baby doll when she was sad.*

"Yes, he's a good boy to sleep for Momma. He sleeps like he's supposed to." She cooed at the doll and touched its plastic face tenderly, as if it were real. For a long time I thought the baby doll was real. But it never made any noise and she left it forgotten in its crib in her room for days at a time. Eventually I realized it was just a baby doll.

Then I'd made the mistake of picking it up and rocking it, too. Momma had been very upset with me. I had gone three days without food, locked in my room.

"Sweet little baby, Momma's joy. I'm gonna go buy you some new toys." She sang the made-up words. She always made up words to this song. I wasn't sure if she didn't know the real words or if she just liked singing about what she was doing.

Then she threw the baby doll across the room and screamed, "Demon child!" over and over again as she stomped her feet. I ran back to my room as fast as I could and prayed she wouldn't come after me.

"Della?" Woods's voice broke into my dream and my eyes snapped open. I looked up into his concerned face.

"You okay? You were breathing hard."

That was all? I smiled. I was okay. I could live with the memories. If the terror didn't come with them. "I'm fine," I assured him, and cuddled against his side. "It was just a memory."

Woods ran his fingers up and down my arm. "Do you want to talk about them? Maybe if you told me, you would stop dreaming them altogether."

I started to say no and stopped. I had been telling people no for years because it sent me into the darkness when I let myself think about it. But I was better now. What if I did tell him my dreams . . . what if it could actually help?

"Okay," I said, not looking up at him. I kept my eyes on his chest. I wasn't scared of the memories now. I just wasn't sure how I was going to open myself up to him that completely. It would make me feel more vulnerable than I had ever felt. He would know my horrors. No one really knew them.

It was time.

Woods tightened his hold on me and I focused on the warmth of his arms. I was safe. Telling him was safe.

"She was rocking the baby doll. She always rocked the baby doll when she was in one of her dark times. She sang to it and made up words to lullabies. I knew, even at five years old, that her singing to a plastic doll was wrong. Something was wrong. So, I would watch her. She never rocked me. Seeing her rock the doll confused me. Why would she rock a plastic baby doll? The baby was a he. She called it a him. She never called it by a name. Just 'sweet baby' and 'baby boy.' That was weird, too, because the boy they'd adopted before me was never a baby when they had him." I stopped a moment and thought about looking up at Woods to see what he was thinking. But I had more to tell and I didn't want to watch his eyes and see his reaction.

"If she ever saw me watching her rock the baby she would yell at me and often hit me. She would tell me to be quiet, that the baby was sleeping. Or to go fix my brother some food and make sure he ate it. I hated making my brother food. I knew he'd never eat it and that it would get old and stinky before she'd finally give in and throw it away. The smell of rotten food permeated our house. I hated the stench." I lay still in Woods's arms. I knew that what I was telling him was disturbing. I knew it would bother him, but it was helping. He had been right. Talking about what I'd lived through with someone who loved me, not just a psychiatrist, helped.

"When she was rocking the baby doll she would eventually realize it was plastic. I never knew what it was she saw but she would start screaming *demon child* and she would throw it across the room like it was on fire. Then she would claw at herself and pull her hair. She would tell the doll she was sorry that she had let him go to the store. She was sorry that she hadn't kept him safe. But then she would point and scream *demon* at it again. I didn't usually watch that part except for once. It terrified me. When she started screaming I would hurry back to my room and close my door. That's what I was dreaming about tonight. One of those moments."

Woods let out a long, shaky breath. "Shit," he whispered, then pressed his face to the top of my head. He didn't say anything else. He just held me. That was what I needed the most.

It didn't feel like I thought it would, opening myself up like that to him. I had always thought that showing someone what was inside, what had been my life, would expose me in a way that would make me unlovable. But I didn't feel that way in Woods's arms. He held me tightly to him and kissed my head. No other words were needed.

My eyes closed and I relaxed in his arms. I had always felt safe with Woods. That wasn't new. But now . . . now I felt like I'd found my anchor. My entire life I'd held on to anything I thought could hold me still and keep me from going under. I had clung to Braden for years, hoping that having her would remind me I was normal. That I wasn't in that house anymore. But even though she loved me, she had never made me feel completely secure. She couldn't give me the grounding I needed. I thought no one would ever be able to give that to me. Not after all I'd seen and lived through. I knew now that it wasn't true. With Woods's arms wrapped around me and the beat of his heart pressed against my chest, I knew he would hold me steady. If I ever fell, I'd have him to catch me.

Woods

I had drunk three cups of coffee that morning to prepare myself for the early tee time I had with Nile. After Della had told me about her dream last night and shared her memories, I hadn't been able to sleep. I'd wanted to hold her and watch her sleep. The idea of her having another dream like that and my not being awake to stop it scared the shit out of me.

That was fucked up. What she'd lived through was more fucked up than I could even imagine. She worried that she wasn't strong enough, but, damn, anyone who had lived through what she had and still functioned normally day to day was strong. Della did more than function. She laughed, she made friends, she enjoyed life, she made me smile, and she completed my world. She was the strongest person I had ever met.

"Sorry I'm late. The girls woke up early and I was trying to get them something to eat so they could watch television and let their mother sleep late," Nile said, interrupting my thoughts.

With his dark hair and blue eyes, he looked so much like Della that it was hard for me not to stare at him. There was no arguing that this man was her father. "No worries. I haven't been here long," I assured him.

"You want a caddy?" I asked. I never used one but most members did.

Nile glanced over at the golf cart I had already pulled around with my clubs and a set from the clubhouse. He had mentioned last night that he hadn't brought his clubs with him.

"No, I think I'd like it to be just us," he said with a smile.

He wanted to talk about Della. I figured as much. Which was why I hadn't already had a caddy on standby.

"All right, then we're ready to go. I have water in the cooler but if you want something more, a cart will be around by the time we get to the third hole. We can order something from it if you prefer."

"Water's great. Too early for anything else," he replied.

I drove us to the first hole. "Della is looking forward to meeting the girls and your wife down at the beach today." They had planned a beach day. Nile was going to join them after our game. I was going to go work and give Della time alone with them.

"The girls can't wait to see Della again. They really took to her. Jillian adores her, too."

I parked the cart. "Della's hard not to adore," I said before getting out.

"Yeah, she is. She's much like her mother . . . uh, Glenda, that way."

I hadn't met Glenda but I wanted to. Della looked like her birth father but she didn't have his personality.

Nile pulled his driver from the bag. "Della seems happy here," he said.

"She is," I replied.

He didn't move to set up his shot. He studied me instead. "You haven't proposed to her. And I couldn't help but notice she didn't make it sound like marriage was in her near future last night when the girls were questioning her."

Not a conversation I had expected to have with him today. I pulled my driver from the bag and tried not to get pissed by this line of questioning. "We haven't talked about marriage yet."

Nile nodded. "I see," he said.

What the hell did "I see" mean? I was going to marry Della.

"I'm going to shoot straight with you, Woods. You're a good man. You have a bright future. When the woman you want to marry walks into your life, you will know it and you will want to be married to her. So, seeing as how you aren't thinking of marriage to Della just yet, I know, as a man, that you aren't sure she's the one for you. I was going to wait but I have decided to ask Della to move to Phoenix and live with us. Jillian is on board with this idea. We stayed up most of last night talking about it. We have an extra bedroom and Della can finish school. She's only twenty. She needs a family around her."

I could hear what he was saying but I felt like I had just stepped outside of myself and was watching this conversation happening. This wasn't real. It couldn't be real. This man was not suggesting taking Della away from me. I shook my head before he finished talking and he stopped midsentence.

"No," was all I managed to say. He had blindsided me. I hadn't expected this.

"No?" he repeated as if he didn't understand that word.

"No," I repeated. "You're not taking Della away from me. I'll follow her. Anywhere she goes I will follow her. She's it for me. She isn't going to Phoenix. She's staying here with me. I'm going to marry her. No, I haven't proposed yet, but I intend to. She just came back to me. She's finally facing the horrors of her past and letting me help her heal. She's mine, Nile. She is mine. She's not going anywhere."

Nile studied me a moment, then he nodded. A smile touched his lips. "That's what I wanted to hear," he said, then turned and walked to the tee as if the conversation were over. It wasn't fucking over until he told me he wasn't asking Della to move to Phoenix.

"What does that mean?" I demanded.

Nile glanced back at me over his shoulder. "You showed passion and determination to keep her. You want her forever. I wanted to make sure. Now I just need to make sure she wants the same thing."

"You mean you lied to me to get me to admit I was going to marry her?" I asked. I wasn't sure I liked this man anymore.

"No. I'm very serious. If Della wants to move to Phoenix with us, then I'm taking her. I will spend every damn dime I have making up for the fact that I was a kid when she was born and didn't know any better. I will give her a family and I'll make sure she feels loved and a part of my family. But I needed to know that if I leave her here, then she'll have someone who loves her with the passion that forever requires."

Wait . . . he was still asking her to move to Phoenix? "Della isn't just mine. I belong to her."

Nile nodded. "Good. If she feels the same way she will tell me no when I ask her to move to Phoenix. If she does, I will know that she has a happy future ahead of her. I will also expect an invitation to the wedding."

"She won't leave me," I said with more force than necessary.

"I guess we will see. Won't we?" he said before giving his complete attention to his swing.

Della

Jasmine may have only been a couple minutes older than Jocelyn but she seemed years older. She laid out on a towel as if she were a teenager and talked to me about name-brand clothing, which I knew nothing about, but I tried hard to follow along.

Jocelyn and July asked me to build a sand castle with them, then we played in the waves until seaweed wrapped around July's leg and sent her screaming to the shore.

Jillian and I talked when the girls gave us a chance, but I preferred playing with them. They were so full of life. Nile had been a good father. They loved him. They all called him Daddy, which I thought was endearing.

"Are you going to come live with us? I heard Daddy talking to Mommy about it late last night. They thought I was sleeping." Jasmine watched me carefully.

I wasn't prepared for that question. She had waited until her mother had gotten up to take July to the restroom. I couldn't figure out why Nile would even think to ask me to come live with them. I was happy here. I had a home.

"I have a home here," I told her.

She nodded. "Yeah, but Daddy said you aren't engaged

and it didn't look like you were going to get engaged. He was thinking you could live with us and go to college. We could be your family."

I was pretty sure Nile had never meant for me to know about this conversation. "I don't think we should be talking about this. If your dad wants me to know about it, then he will talk to me about it."

Jasmine rolled over and looked up at me. "He's going to. Just so you know."

Was this kid really nine? She acted like she was fifteen.

"Here comes Daddy now," she said with a smirk.

I glanced back over my shoulder to see Nile walking toward us in a pair of blue and yellow plaid shorts and a white polo shirt. He looked like he'd just walked off the golf course.

"Daddy," Jocelyn squealed from next to her attempts at another sand castle, and went running to him. He reached down and picked her up and hugged her. Then he pretended to care that she'd gotten sand on him. It was cute.

"Hey, Daddy, what did you shoot?"

"Seventy-nine. I'm rusty. Woods shot a seventy. It was impressive."

I was glad that they'd gotten to spend time together. Nile and his family were going home tomorrow. I wasn't sure if, or when, I would see them again.

"How have you girls fared out here on the beach?" he asked, sitting down beside me.

"Other than the time July got seaweed on her leg, I think we've done brilliantly," I told him.

Jasmine laughed. "It was epic."

Nile looked over at her and grinned. "I can only imagine." He looked around. "Where are Jillian and July?"

"Restroom," I explained.

We sat there a few minutes and didn't say much. Jocelyn kept calling out to us to look at her sand castle, but other than that we all remained quiet.

Finally, Jasmine and July returned and July plopped down in Nile's lap and told him every second of everything he'd missed. He listened to her like he was hearing the most intriguing story ever told. She expected it, too. She was secure in the fact that her dad wanted to listen to her. He wanted to know what she had to say.

"Girls, let's go down and get our feet wet and leave Daddy to talk to Della for a few minutes," Jillian said, standing up and holding her hand out for July to take.

I glanced at Jasmine, who was giving me an *I told you so* look before she stood up and followed her mother and sisters down to the water.

"Why don't you and I go for a walk?" Nile suggested, standing up and holding out his hand for me to take so he could help me up. I didn't need his help but he was wired to be a gentleman, so I let him.

We began walking and I waited for him to say something.

"I want you to move back to Phoenix with us, Della. We have an extra bedroom over the bonus room. It would give you privacy and you would have a separate entrance into the house. You could go to school out there and we could all get to know each other better. The girls love you. Jillian thinks you're great. We all want you to come live with us, though I know you have a life here."

"Della!" Woods's voice broke into Nile's surprising offer and I stopped and turned around to see Woods running toward me. What was he doing here?

"Well, I'll be damned," Nile said beside me with an amused tone. I didn't have time to focus on him and his offer. Woods looked upset.

"Woods?" I searched his face to see if there was something wrong. Was someone hurt?

"Don't leave me," he said, grabbing my arms and taking a deep breath like he had been running for a few miles.

"What are you talking about? I'm not leaving you."

He looked over at Nile, then back at me with determination in his eyes. "I love you. You're my one. My all-in. Don't leave me."

Had Nile told him he was going to ask me to leave with him? If he had, then why would Woods even think I would go? Had I made him feel that insecure about us? Of course I had. I had run off and left him with nothing but a letter. I reached up and grabbed Woods's face and looked into his eyes. I needed him to hear me.

"I'm not leaving you. Ever. You'll have to send me packing to get me to leave, and then I plan on fighting back. I will handcuff myself to you and refuse to budge. Nothing will make me leave. Nothing." I brushed my thumbs over his cheekbones; it was really unfair how they were so perfect.

"He's going to ask you to go to Phoenix," he said, watching my face.

"I know. He just did. Doesn't mean I'm going," I told him, and smiled up at his beautiful, troubled face.

"So, you're not leaving me?" he asked.

I shook my head and dropped my hands from his face and turned to look at Nile. "The fact that you and Jillian and the girls would be willing to accept me into your family so easily is humbling. I am touched. I want to get to know you and them. But I won't be leaving Rosemary. I won't be leaving Woods. He's my family. The people here are my family. I don't need another one. I have what I need here."

Nile didn't look hurt or ready to argue. Instead, I could see a pleased expression light up his face. "As much as I wanted you to come live with me and give us a chance to become a family, I'm thankful that you have someone who loves you like that," he said, nodding his head at Woods. "I can trust him to take care of you and know you're okay. I didn't take care of you when you needed it. Now that I've found you, I want you to be happy and safe. I believe this man can give you that."

Woods pulled me against him.

"He can. He does that and so much more," I replied.

Woods

It was time for the end-of-summer beach bonfire. The past two months had been perfect. Della was sharing more and more of her past with me and her dreams were starting to completely go away. She'd woken me up in the middle of the night the week before last to tell me she'd had a dream about us. That we'd been having sex on the kitchen table. She'd been so excited to have a dream that didn't contain the horrors of her past that she'd been ready to play it out in real life.

It was a pretty damn good way to wake up.

I watched as she held Nate and danced around with him as the music pumped through the speakers. Blaire was in Rush's lap and they were watching Della with their son. She was beautiful. I wanted to see her dance around and laugh with our baby. I wanted her to have a child to love the way she was never loved. I wanted to know we had created something from the love that bound us so tightly together.

"She's happy," Jace said.

"She's perfect," I replied.

Jace laughed and slapped me on the back. "Just go ahead and do it. You know you want to. Put that little ring on her finger."

"I'm planning it. Has to be special."

Jace sighed. "Yeah, I'm planning it, too. Bethy and I've had a hard summer but things are looking better. She's stopped running off to bars. I think she just had a dark time there for a while. She's been spending time with Blaire and Della again. That helps."

Jace hadn't shown up on my doorstep upset about Bethy in two months. I was hoping things were better. "Good. Glad you two are working it out."

"Oh, shit. Is that Nan?" Jace said, pointing her out to me. "I thought she left and went to Paris for the summer. Seeing Nan is gonna send Grant into a tailspin again." Grant wasn't at the party; he was out of town. That was happening a lot lately. He would show up for a couple of days then leave again. I was just glad he wasn't wasting time with Nan.

"Grant has moved on. If Nan's back, then he'll be fine. She was a bad mistake. He knows that now."

Jace let out a low whistle. "She's with August Schweep. What, did she bring him back from Paris with her?"

"No. August is our new golf pro. We needed more than just Marco. When August hurt his rotator cuff his pro career was over. He wants to retire here, so he bought the Spencer house. He's working for me now."

"Looks like Nan is all over that."

"Good. At least it's not Grant."

Jace snorted. "Ain't that the truth."

I was going to get Della and take her for a walk. The dark beach was a great place to get her alone. Turning, I glanced out over the water and saw Bethy staggering out to the waves. She knew better than that. There was a red flag up. Had been all week. The riptides were intense and it was dark. You don't swim in the gulf in the dark.

"Jace, man, what's Bethy doing?" I asked, afraid to take my eyes off her.

"What is she doing now? She was drinking tequila shots earlier and I cut her off. She'd had enough . . . shit!"

"She's getting too deep," I said, taking a step toward the water. Jace took off running toward the water. I followed behind him. I heard someone scream from the crowd as Bethy's head went under the water. *No.* This couldn't be happening.

Jace dove into the waves and took off toward her. I pulled my shirt off, afraid it would slow me down, before I dove in after him. I wasn't letting my best friend go into this alone.

Bethy's gurgling scream filled the air.

"Relax, baby! Relax. Don't fight it. Please don't fight it. You'll go under and won't have the strength to rise back up," Jace was yelling as he swam toward her.

I saw him grab her just as the deathly pull of a rip current grabbed him. This wasn't happening. No.

"I need you to take her, Woods!" Jace yelled over the water's roar.

"Give me both your hands!" I shouted.

"*No!* Take her. I got this. Take her, dammit! It's strong!" Jace yelled.

How was I supposed to take her and leave him out there? "Come with me, Jace!" I demanded.

"Woods, listen to me—" His head went under and he came back up as he held a panicking Bethy in his arms. "You have to take her or we'll all die. I'm not gonna let her drown. Help me!"

I nodded. I had to do this. He could get out of the current.

He was strong and he was smart. We had grown up knowing how to fight rip currents. I reached for Bethy as she screamed Jace's name.

"I love you," he told her as he let her go. She cried as she clung to my arms.

"Don't say that!" I yelled at him. "You're getting out of this. Don't fucking say that."

"Just get her out of here!" he yelled, pushing her away from him and toward me as he held on to her arm.

I could feel the pull getting closer. If I stayed here much longer I was going to get pulled into it, too. I wrapped my hand around Bethy's arm and pulled her out of the current, then tucked her under my arm and I started swimming back to shore.

Rush came swimming up to us and relief surged through me. I was going to be able to help Jace.

"Give her to me," Rush said as he reached for Bethy.

"Go get him," she cried as Rush pulled her from my arms.

I didn't wait for them to leave before I turned back around to get Jace.

But Jace wasn't there.

I glanced back at the shore to see if he'd made his way back up there and I'd missed it, but all I saw was Rush carrying Bethy out of the water.

I turned back to the dark waves. I was met with silence. Nothing.

He was just here. I just saw him. He isn't gone. It didn't happen that fast.

I went under and forced my eyes open in the salty water, but all I could see was the darkness. I needed light. I reached around me, feeling for anything. My lungs started to burn. Kicking up, I broke the surface and took a deep breath. I heard my name from the shore. They were yelling for me. I also heard Jace's name. I couldn't go back without him.

I went back under. I had to find Jace. I couldn't lose Jace. Not like this. Not now. We were supposed to be grumpy old men together. I fought back the panic starting to set in with each second that I couldn't find him. I swam underwater and fought the pull of the current as I reached out for some sign of him. Anything I could get my hands on.

When my lungs couldn't take it anymore, I swam back to the top, only to be taken back under by a wave before I could breathe. I wasn't going down like this. I had to find Jace.

Two arms grabbed ahold of me and jerked me to the surface as I started gasping for air and coughing.

"Dammit, Woods. Come on. You're gonna drown in this. He's gone, man. He's gone. I'm not letting you drown, too." Rush's words sent a shock through my system. *He's gone? No. No! He isn't gone.* I fought against Rush's hold on me.

"Stop it! Della is up there in a crumpled mess, crying. Do you want to leave her? Is that what you want? To leave her like this?"

Della. Oh God. Della. I couldn't leave her. But I'd lost Jace. I had lost Jace.

Rush pulled us out of the waves and when my feet hit the sand he let me go. We stood there staring at each other and breathing hard. We knew what had happened and what we were going to face. I would have been gone, too, if Rush hadn't come after me. I would have left Della behind.

I turned to see her getting up from the sand where she had

been on her knees. Her face was red and soaked with tears. All she said was, "Woods," before she threw herself into my arms.

I watched in a daze as Blaire stood holding a hysterical Bethy. Sirens wailed in the distance. Sobs and cries filled the beach. And I stood there. Della clung to me. Her sobs eased but her hold never did.

Rush walked over to take his crying son from Nan's arms. He held him to his chest, and although he wasn't crying the loss and pain were in his eyes.

Me . . . I just felt empty.

Della

I had thought that I knew terror. That I knew fear. I had seen my mother lying in a pool of her own blood. That was fear. But seeing Woods out in that water going under and not coming up—that had been all-consuming terror. Nothing compared to that. Nothing.

Jace hadn't come back up, though. My chest hurt so bad I couldn't take deep breaths. Jace was gone. I had seen it happen, and the broken sobs coming from Bethy as Blaire held her on the sand only ripped through me harder. I couldn't imagine that. That had almost been me. That could have been me on that sand, knowing the man I loved wasn't coming back to me.

Woods's body shuddered and reality started to hit me. The idea of losing him had been all I could think about. But he'd been out there for a reason. He had gone to save his best friend. He'd watched his best friend be pulled under, unable to save him.

I tightened my hold on him. How was he going to survive this?

Bethy continued to wail and Woods's body went stiff. He was strung so tight he was trembling.

213

"Get her the fuck out of my sight!" he roared. I jumped back, startled by the angry hate that laced his words. His eyes were glaring and focused on someone behind me. I turned to see that he was looking at Bethy.

Blaire's face went pale and Bethy cried harder.

"I said to get her selfish, trashy ass off my beach! *Now!*"

I swallowed hard and watched as Bethy looked up at him with big, pain-filled eyes.

Rush was behind Blaire, helping Bethy stand up. I heard him telling her they needed to take Bethy somewhere else. Woods was yelling at Bethy. He was blaming her.

"Woods?" I was almost afraid of the man in front of me. He swung his gaze to mine and there was an emptiness in them I couldn't reach.

"She killed him," he said simply.

Maybe she had. She had gone into the water and almost drowned. Jace had died saving her. But she had been drinking.

"She loved him," I said.

Woods shook his head. "No. She didn't love him. You don't do what she did and call that love."

I glanced back and saw Blaire lead Bethy up to the board-walk. The cops would want to question her. She wouldn't be able to go far.

"Woods, she lost him, too. We all did," Thad said as he stood watching Woods, afraid to get too close.

"I lost him because he wanted me to save her worthless, drunk ass. I did what he wanted and I lost him." Woods's voice was cold and emotionless.

Headlights lit up the beach as ambulances and police cars arrived. Paramedics swarmed the stretch of sand and I watched as they were told by several of the people at the party what they had seen. A paramedic approached Woods.

"You were one of the people who were in the water?" he asked.

"Yes," Woods replied.

"We need to check you out," he said.

"No."

I watched as the paramedic started to argue and stepped between him and Woods. "He's fine. If I think he needs medical attention I will make sure he gets it. Please, he needs to be left alone."

The man looked up at Woods and then back at me. "Okay," he said, then turned away.

"I'm not leaving until they've found him," Woods said.

I turned around and reached for his hand. He laced his fingers through mine. "Okay," I said. "We'll stay right here."

"You'll stay with me?" he asked.

"I'm not leaving your side."

"Thank you."

◈

We sat there for the next four hours. Rush had brought Woods a blanket from one of the ambulances to keep him from getting cold since he was soaking wet. He didn't say anything, he just dropped it on his shoulders. Rush had been out there, too. He had been the reason Woods hadn't drowned. They had both lived this nightmare.

After the police questioned Bethy, Darla came and took her home. Blaire took Nate and went home at Rush's insistence. The crowd had thinned. Helicopters spotlighted the dark water and boats searched in vain. It was impossible to see in the dark.

Woods sat there beside me, not letting go of my hand and staring at the water. Watching them look for Jace. He wanted Jace's body found. I understood that. He didn't want to leave the beach until he knew Jace wasn't out there alone.

Finally, the helicopters left. The boats went away. The paramedics packed up and drove off. A police officer tried to get us to leave but they weren't going to argue with the owner of the Kerrington Club. They finally left us.

We weren't alone, though. Rush stood off in the distance, his hands in the pockets of his jeans. At some point he'd changed clothes. He was staring off at the dark water, too. I kept thinking this was a dream I would wake up from, but it never ended. I glanced over to our left and Thad sat there on the sand with his arms wrapped around his legs and his knees bent, like a little boy who was lost.

They all hurt.

And there was nothing I could do. Nothing anyone could do.

The sound of the ocean crashing against the shore wasn't soothing like it had once been. It now felt like a taunt. Reminding us that it was stronger. It was in control.

Someone else moved in the darkness and I watched as Grant came running down the boardwalk. He hadn't been at the party. I never knew if he was in town or somewhere else. The guy never stayed in one place.

He stopped at Rush and Rush turned his eyes to look at him. They stood there for a moment, then Grant hung his head and dropped to his knees.

It was morning when the searchers found Jace's body washed up one mile down the shore.

Woods

I stood under the shower spray and let Della wash me. She washed my hair and body so methodically and thoroughly. She never said a word. She didn't ask me questions. She was just there beside me. I needed her to stay there. If she left me I was afraid the reality would set in and I couldn't let it. It hurt too fucking much.

"You're clean," Della said softly, opening the shower door and stepping out. She picked up a towel and began to dry me. And I let her.

When she was finished she wrapped the towel around herself and pressed a kiss to my chest. "Go, get in bed. You need to sleep," she told me.

She turned to walk away and I reached out and grabbed her hand. "Don't leave me." The words sounded more like pleading. They didn't sound like me at all.

She shook her head. "I'm not. I just need to get dry. I'll be in bed in a minute," she assured me.

"I'll wait," I told her as I stood there. I was scared of my own nightmares now. I couldn't lie down and face them without her with me.

"Okay. I'll hurry," she said. I saw the sadness and pain in her eyes.

She dried off her body and wrapped the towel around her hair, then went to the dresser. When she opened it and pulled out a pair of panties, I moved toward her.

"No. Don't wear clothes." I wanted her in my arms just like this. I wanted her warmth to reach my empty coldness inside. She was the only reason I was still alive. If it hadn't been for her I wouldn't have stopped until I'd drowned, too.

"Okay."

She reached for my hand and took me over to the bed. I lay down and she climbed in beside me, then pulled the covers up over us. *If Rush hadn't come back I wouldn't be here now.* I held on to her tighter.

She would've been here without me. I didn't want to think about that. Not being there to protect her. To hold her. Not being there to spend forever with her.

"I came back for you." My voice sounded hoarse.

She tilted back her head and looked up at me. "Thank you."

I didn't say anything else. I wasn't sure what to say. Within minutes, my eyes were too heavy to hold open and the smooth heat of Della's skin gave me the comfort I needed to fall asleep.

⬦

When I opened my eyes, I stared at the ceiling. It was late afternoon. I could tell by the sunlight through the windows. Della's slow, even breathing told me she was still asleep. I hadn't dreamed. Thank God.

I hadn't wanted to dream. It all replayed over and over again in my head. Jace was going to propose to Bethy. He'd been ready to spend his life with her. We had been right there together and everything had been fine.

Then Bethy had changed all that. She'd turned a summer night we were all supposed to enjoy together into a nightmare. One that would never leave us. One that we would all relive over and over the rest of our lives. Remembering the helpless feeling of knowing he was gone and there was nothing we could do to bring him back.

I had lived on this beach my entire life. We had seen more than one death from the water but it had never been a death that impacted me. It had never been someone I loved. It had never been real.

It was real now.

Della moved in my arms and I held her tighter. She was my glue right now. Being able to touch her was keeping me together. Last night she'd sat right there on that beach, refusing to let go of my hand.

When they had found his body she had wrapped her arms around me and used every ounce of strength to hold me as they covered him and took him. I couldn't have made it without her. Holding her reminded me that I was alive. I hadn't drowned. When she walked away from me or left me for even a moment, I was under that wave again, being sucked away and unable to fight it.

"Woods?" Della's concerned voice brought me out of my head and I blinked, then focused on her face. "I'm here," she said simply, and brushed the hair from my forehead.

I reached up and touched her face. I didn't have words just yet. I couldn't talk about it. I just needed her near me.

She moved her body over mine until she was on top of me.

She straddled my waist and pressed small kisses to my neck and shoulders. This was her way of easing my pain. I could feel it in each gentle brush of her lips. Her hips moved down until I could feel her wet heat slide over me. The contact was all I needed to be ready.

Della lifted her hips and I slid into her with ease. When I was completely inside she leaned forward and rested her head on my heart. We stayed there a few moments. Joined in a way that only she could achieve.

When her hips began to rock against me she didn't seek my mouth or get frantic with her need for release. She just loved me. She used her body to love me and hold me in the most intimate way.

I wrapped my arms around her and held her against me. We moved with each other in a perfect rhythm that was selfless. Its purpose was to heal and comfort. When Della's warmth began to tighten around me and her body started to tremble, I cried out her name and she followed me.

After I filled her with my release she didn't move from me. She held me inside her as we stared into each other's eyes. All the pain and devastation of last night was there. We didn't need words.

"He would have wanted you to come back," she finally said.

"I know," I told her.

She pressed a kiss to my cheek. "He loved you."

"I know."

Della

The beach was empty. It was the middle of the day in August and the beach was empty. Almost forty-eight hours had passed since Jace drowned. Tourists had already gone back to their lives. It was the locals who were left to mourn. Woods hadn't wanted to leave the house yet. I was going to have to make him eventually but I didn't want to push him.

I thought I should call Tripp but I didn't know what to say. He was probably with family. I would see him tomorrow at the funeral. I knew that. I just felt like I should call. Say something. He would mourn this just as hard as Woods. Jace was his cousin. He was like his little brother.

Then there was Bethy. I hadn't called Bethy. I wasn't sure how Woods would react to that. He obviously blamed her for Jace's death. I was afraid he always would. I wasn't sure if forgiveness could be granted to her for this. Not from Woods.

Rush had dropped by that morning to check on Woods. He had still been sleeping. I'd told him I'd let Woods know he came by. Grant had stopped by an hour later. His red-rimmed eyes reminded me of Woods's hollow look.

Woods hadn't been awake then, either. He had slept until eleven. When he realized I wasn't in bed with him he had jumped up and come after me. He hadn't said anything but pulled me into his lap. We had sat there for an hour in silence.

Finally, I had told him about Rush and Grant stopping by. Then I'd convinced him to get dressed and eat something. I turned from my view of the gulf and walked back into the kitchen to check on the chicken Parmesan I had put in the oven.

Woods walked out of the bedroom freshly showered and dressed in jeans and a T-shirt. "I need to go to the office today," he said.

"Lunch is almost ready. Can you eat first?" I really wanted him to eat.

"After we eat I want us both to go. I want you with me."

I didn't ask why, I just nodded. Right now he seemed to need me. I would be whatever he needed me to be. It was my turn to be the strong one. This time I would be his shoulder to lean on.

"It smells good," he said as he walked around the counter to kiss me. He was doing that a lot lately too. More than normal. Sometimes they were desperate, hungry kisses that led to more, but most of the time they were kisses that held words he couldn't say.

"I need to go to the store. I worked with what we had," I explained as I pulled the chicken out of the oven. I kept myself busy fixing us each a plate and toasting some bread and buttering it.

"Soda?" I asked him.

"Do we have sweet tea?" he asked.

We did. I had made it that morning. I fixed him a glass while he carried our food to the table.

"Thank you," he said as I set the drink down in front of him.

"You're welcome."

He reached up and grabbed my hand. "No. Thank you for being exactly what I needed and knowing when I wanted to speak and when I didn't." That was one of the longest sentences he'd said since we'd come home from the beach.

"I will always be whatever you need me to be," I said simply before taking my seat.

We ate for a few minutes in silence.

"I need to see his parents . . . and Tripp. He's called my phone twice. I should see him, too."

"Okay."

"I want you to go with me."

"Okay," I agreed.

Woods looked out at the water. "Do you know when the funeral is?"

"Yes. Rush said it was tomorrow at two."

His jaw worked as he stared out the window. "Will Bethy be there?"

"Yes. I'm sure she will be," I replied.

His jaw continued to shift like he was clenching his teeth.

I reached over and took his hand. "Woods. She loved him, too. She made a mistake that she'll have to live with for the rest of her life, but she did love him. You know that."

"I can't forgive her," he said.

"I understand that. But remember, he loved her. He loved her enough to die for her. She's suffering. Don't doubt that. She's suffering because she knows why this happened. You can hate her but try to remind yourself of the pain she has to be going through. And that Jace loved her more than he loved himself."

Woods didn't say anything; he just sat there, letting me hold his hand while he stared out the window.

◇

Everyone in Rosemary was at the funeral. There were more people there than I'd ever seen at any event in town. Bethy was lifeless. Her face was pale and her cheeks were hollowed. She stood beside her aunt Darla and a man I assumed was her father. Jace's parents I had seen a few times at the club. His mother's eyes were red and swollen as she clung to his father's arm. Tripp stood to the side of them. He was dressed in a dark suit. You couldn't see his tattoos and he looked nothing like a biker bartender but more like the Ivy League graduate that he would have been if he hadn't run from his parents' plans for him.

Woods held on to my hand like it was his lifeline. He hadn't let it go since we arrived. Rush also held Blaire's hand just as tightly. Nate wasn't with them today.

Grant stood on the other side of Rush, his hands tucked in his front pockets and his face pinched in a permanent frown. It looked like he was trying not to cry.

The others were there, too, but I couldn't see them from where we were standing.

Each one of them had had an impact on the others' lives.

They all had stories.

They had all loved, and many had lost.

They had expected to grow up and become adults together. Get married and let their kids play together.

They'd planned on being the next generation in Rosemary.

What they hadn't planned on was losing one of their own. Losing a member of their tight group. They hadn't seen their future minus one. Death hadn't touched them before. Not like this. Not one of them.

Everything was about to change.

Bethy

My entire life I had loved the sound of the waves. The natural beauty of the gulf. I was proud to live in such a special place.

But that had all changed.

The crashing waves were cruel. It had been two weeks since the water had taken Jace from me. Two weeks since I cheated death and it had taken the man I loved instead.

"It should have been me," I screamed at the water. I wanted it to know it had messed up and taken the wrong life.

"He wouldn't have agreed with you."

I didn't want to hear that voice. Not now. Not now that Jace was gone. I wanted him to go away.

"No one should have died, Bethy. And Jace made sure it wasn't you. It wasn't the water who took the wrong person. Jace made that decision." I wanted to cover my ears like a child and scream at him to go away. I didn't want him here. Why was he still here? He knew it was my fault. He knew this was all my fault, yet he didn't look at me with hate in his eyes the way Woods did.

"Go away," I said without looking back at him.

"I'm not leaving again."

Those were not words I wanted to hear right now. Maybe

five years ago I would have loved to have heard Tripp Newark tell me he was staying in Rosemary, but not now. Any and all feelings I had for Tripp had died the day I walked out of the abortion clinic Aunt Darla had taken me to, with an ache in my chest where my heart used to be.

"You can do what you want. Just stay away from me," I snapped, finally turning my angry glare on him. He was still just as beautiful as he had been when I was sixteen and stupid. He had said pretty words and I had believed him.

"I will for now. But I've been running for five years, Bethy."

It wasn't my fault he had been running. He had left me without an explanation or apology. He hadn't answered my phone calls. Nothing. Not even the message I'd left him after I had killed our baby. I had been devastated. He hadn't even called me back then.

"*I loved him!*" I yelled, and pointed my finger at Tripp. "*I loved Jace!* It was *real*! Damn you! It was real. Don't come to me and tell me you're coming back. Don't tell me you're tired of running. I don't give a motherfucking shit! I loved him." My angry screams had turned to sobs, but I didn't care. He'd asked for this. He should have stayed away from me.

"I loved him," I said one more time before turning to walk away.

"I loved him, too. He was like my brother. He was everything I wasn't. He was good. He was honest. He was strong. He deserved you."

I stopped and let the pain slice through me. *He's gone. How could he be gone?*

"I'm sorry, Bethy. I'm sorry that I just left you that summer. I was young and stupid. My parents wanted things for me I didn't want and I was scared of becoming my dad. So I ran like hell. I wanted to tell you. Dammit, I wanted to take you with me, but you were sixteen years old. You were an even bigger kid than I was. What was an eighteen-year-old trust fund brat going to do taking care of a sixteen-year-old?"

It was the past. Nothing he said made up for what he'd done. It was over. I had let it go and buried it and moved on.

"I was in love with you, Bethy. You were the first girl I ever loved. You've been the only girl I've ever loved. I never wanted to hurt you. When Jace was smart enough to fall in love with you I knew you'd be okay. He would give you everything you deserved."

"Shut up!" I snapped, spinning around and glaring at him "Just shut up! He didn't know! He loved me and he trusted me and he didn't know. I never told him. I wasn't worthy of him. I was never worthy of him. I was a liar. I'm tainted. I'm dirty."

Tripp took a step toward me. "No, you're not. Just because you trusted me with your love and then gave me your virginity . . . Bethy, that doesn't make you tainted or dirty. What we had wasn't wrong. It was real. I was too young to deal with it but it was very fucking real. It never left me."

Giving him my virginity was stupid. I had been a good girl then. Sex had equaled love to me. But Tripp had changed all that. He had turned me into something that Jace saved me from. The girl Tripp had destroyed, Jace had salvaged and cherished.

"No. Loving you was stupid, not wrong. Trusting you with my virginity was a mistake, not dirty. But killing the baby that we created because you didn't care enough to return my calls . . . that's what made me unworthy of someone like Jace."

I turned and walked away. This time he didn't try to stop me.

Della

I sat in the window of Woods's office and watched him read over some new contracts he needed to sign with a distribu- tor that I had found for the clothing line in the clubhouse. What we had was for an older crowd. The members of the Kerrington Club weren't all fifty and above.

He hadn't wanted me out of his sight for longer than a few minutes. It had been two weeks since the funeral and he was still clingy. It was easing up each day, but he still needed me close by. We were also having sex more often than normal, and that was a whole lot of sex.

Blaire had called and invited me over for lunch today at one. That was Nate's nap time, so she was hoping we could meet at her house. Bethy was also invited. She wasn't working or showing up anywhere anymore. Blaire was worried about her and I was, too. Woods still wouldn't talk about her.

"Blaire has invited me to lunch today at her house at one. Are you okay with me going?" Normally I wouldn't have felt like I had to ask Woods's permission to eat lunch, but with his need for me to be close to him at all times, I wanted to check and make sure.

He looked up from his contract and frowned. I could see

the sadness in his eyes and I almost wished I hadn't asked him and had just told Blaire no.

"I'm sorry, Della."

I stood up. "For what?"

"For making you think you have to ask me to go somewhere. These past couple of weeks I've been needy, and I'm sorry I've done that to you."

I pulled his chair back and straddled his lap, then grabbed both of his shoulders. "Do not apologize to me. Not for that. You needed me and I was able to be what you needed. I was the strong one this time. Not you. Me. I got to be the one to hold your hand. It was my turn to show you how much I love you. So, don't apologize for that."

Woods grinned. He hadn't grinned since before the accident. He lifted his hand and traced my jaw. "You're straddling my lap in a skirt. I want you to go but I'm also thinking about your panties and wondering if they're wet, or if I can get them wet. Hurry and stand up and get away from me before I do something that changes your plans."

Laughing, I jumped out of his lap. "Not that I wouldn't enjoy you checking to see if you could get my panties wet, because I assure you that you could, but Blaire seemed to really want to do lunch."

Woods nodded. "Go eat lunch with her. I'll be fine."

I blew him a kiss that he caught and pressed to his lips. Then I stepped through the door and closed it behind me.

"I heard laughter. It was nice," Vince said from his desk.

I nodded. "He's better," I told him.

"Because of you," he replied.

I just smiled because I knew he was right. I had helped Woods. It had been me.

◇

Blaire opened the door with Nate on her hip. His small hand was fisted in her long platinum hair and he was tugging pretty hard on it.

"Come in," she said with her head tilted in his direction. "Let me detangle myself and get this one in bed and I'll be right back. There's glasses and tea on the table in the kitchen. *Oh!* Nate, that hurts Mommy."

I tried not to laugh but a giggle leaked out.

She grinned and rolled her eyes. "He likes my hair. I'm going to end up bald because he's pulled it all out."

"Go save yourself. I'll get a drink," I told her, and she flashed me an appreciative smile and headed for the staircase. It was a grand, elaborate set of stairs. The whole house was pretty fabulous. It had been Rush's before Blaire. His dad had bought it for him when he was a kid. His mother used to live there when she was in town, but he wasn't on speaking terms with her at the moment.

I walked through the house and stopped to look at the life-sized portrait of Nate above the fireplace in the drawing room. His hair was going to be as pale as his mother's, or at least it looked like it now. The longer it got, the blonder it was.

The kitchen was at the other end of a long hallway with really high ceilings. There were framed photos of the three of them covering the walls. They weren't professional pictures but casual family photos of them playing at the beach or opening gifts at Christmas. There was even one with Rush on a slide with Nate in his lap. He so didn't look like the kind of guy to go down a slide.

Once I got to the kitchen, I fixed myself a glass of tea. The pantry door stood open and I walked over and peeked inside. I had heard about the hidden room under the stairs that you got to through the pantry. It had been where Rush had stuck Blaire when she first came to Rosemary looking for her dad.

Smiling, I wondered if they ever went in that room . . . to remember.

The doorbell rang again and Blaire's footsteps echoed as she came down the stairs. I had wondered if Bethy would come. I hadn't seen her anywhere else so I wasn't sure she would show up, even though Blaire was her best friend.

Both women walked into the room and Bethy's sad, empty eyes met mine. I set my glass down and went over to hug her. She looked like she needed a hug.

"I've missed you," I told her.

She wrapped her arms weakly around me. "Thanks," she sniffled.

"No crying. We're going to eat the cookies I made and not think about calories, and we're going to talk," Blaire announced as she picked up a covered tray, walked over to the table, and set it down.

I wasn't sure if this was going to work, but Blaire looked pretty determined. I watched Bethy as she tried to gather herself and took a seat across from me.

"Okay, so maybe we need to cry first," Blaire said as she saw Bethy's face crumple. "Talk to us. We're here to listen."

Bethy lifted her eyes and shook her head. "No, I'm tired of crying. I'm tired of being sad. I just want to be able to smile again."

"We haven't lost the man we love but we both have lost

people we love. I've lost my mother and my sister. Della lost her mother. We know it hurts and we want you to scream and yell, whatever you have to do to get it out. Then you need to eat cookies and think of funny stories that make you laugh. Think about things that Jace did to make you laugh. Remember him in the good ways. They will overcome the bad memory of that night. I promise you, they will."

Woods

Jimmy had called to tell me I needed to get Grant from the bar. He had drunk too much and was now calling my new golf pro a douchebag. Not a good thing. He'd regret that tomorrow.

I walked past Jimmy, who was shaking his head with an amused grin on his face. Grant was leaning on the bar, trying to convince the new bartender that he was a congressman and demanding another drink.

"I got this," I told the new guy, who looked very relieved.

Grant spun around and almost fell over a stool. "Hey, Woods! It's you. Get me another shot, buddy," he slurred. Grant only called people *buddy* when he was drinking.

"Not a chance in hell," I replied. "Come on, you're going home. You're done for the night."

Grant jerked his arm out of my grasp. "I don't wanna go home. I wanna stay here. I like it here. It's better here. If I go back to my place"—he lowered his voice, although he was still talking really loudly—"she will come."

"Who is she?" I asked, grabbing his arm and jerking him up. I started pushing him toward the door before he could protest this time.

"She is *she*," he said, whispering loudly again.

"She is she? Really? Man, how much have you had to drink?"

Once we were outside, Grant looked around and realized we had been walking. "Aww, damn. You tricked me. We left."

"Why don't you want to go to your place? You need to sleep this off."

Grant looked around us like he was looking for someone who might be hiding and waiting for him to tell a highly important secret.

"She's Nan. Always Nan. And she's pissed. When she gets pissed she gets possessive, then naughty, then she does things and I end up letting her, but now I don't want to let her 'cause I don't even like her. So I can't go home."

Nothing he had said made sense except that he didn't like Nan. Neither did the rest of the world. I was pretty damn sure there was a Twitter hashtag that said #NanHater.

"You want to crash in one of the rooms here?" I asked him as he stumbled and sat down on a bench.

"Can I? She can't find me here. Can she?"

I was pretty sure I hadn't seen him this drunk since boarding school. Nan had done a number on him. "You would think by now you would have learned your lesson about messing around with Nan. She's poison. Why even go near her?"

Grant let out a loud sigh and leaned forward.

"Do not puke on the damn brick. It's a country club, dickhead, not a bar."

He lifted his head and his eyes were glassy. "It ain't Nan that's making me drink. It's her. She's so damn . . . so damn . . . hell, I don't know what she is. She messed up my head. She fucked me over, literally. She won't see me. Won't talk to me.

Nothing. She's guarded like the damn queen. Bunch of damn rock stars act like I'm a problem. I'm not a problem. I just want to see her. I need to explain."

What the hell was he talking about? "I'm lost, dude. You're not making sense anymore. Come on, let's get you a room."

"She's got these legs that go on forever. Lots of legs . . . lots of 'em. They're soft. So fucking soft," he muttered as I jerked him up and walked him over to my truck.

"Nan?"

Grant spit. "Fuck no. I told you this ain't about Nan. She's the evil bitch that fucked it up. She fucks up everything."

I put him in and closed the door, then got in on my side and rolled down the windows. "If you need to hurl do it outside of my truck," I told him before cranking the engine.

"She's got these legs," he said again.

"Yeah, you told me."

"You don't understand, they're like legs from fucking heaven."

Someone had done a number on him. I was thankful it wasn't Nan. That was the only thing I was thankful for at the moment. If I could get him out of my truck without his puking, I'd be thankful for that, too.

"She was a virgin," he whispered.

Wait . . . what? "Now I know we aren't talking about Nan."

Grant leaned his head back on the leather seat. "A virgin. She didn't tell me, either. Now she won't talk to me. I need her to talk to me."

So Grant took a virgin and some rock stars are holding her captive. That doesn't make any . . . oh shit.

"Grant, are you talking about Harlow?"

"Yeah, who the fuck did you think I was talking about?"

That might just be worse than Nan.

Yeah . . . it's definitely worse than Nan.

He was in deep shit. Nan would never let that happen. Ever.

Two months later . . .

Della

Braden was pregnant. I had hung up with her over ten minutes ago but I hadn't moved from the swing on the porch. I continued to swing. I needed to let this process. *Braden . . . a mommy. My Braden. Wow . . .*

The door to the house opened and Woods stepped outside. "You off the phone?" he asked as he walked over to the swing.

"Yeah," I replied, scooting over so he could sit down with me.

"What is Braden up to?" he asked as he put his arm around me and pulled me over to his side.

"She's . . . she's pregnant." It was hard to even say it. I had always imagined Braden as a mom. She would make an excellent one, but just knowing that she was about to start another new step in life was a surprise.

"That's good, right?" Woods asked.

I smiled and nodded. I guess in the moment I took to process, I looked upset. "Yes, it's wonderful. They've been trying for a while now, apparently. I didn't know. She hadn't said anything. But she's now three months along and they heard the heartbeat yesterday. She feels it's safe to tell people now."

Woods pushed the swing with his feet so I curled mine back behind me and let him do the work. "She'll be a wonderful mother," I told him.

"I agree with you. She's pretty damn fierce when she loves someone."

I laughed and looked up at him. "Yes, she is."

Woods bent down and kissed the tip of my nose. "I love you."

"I love you more," I said in reply. That was always his line. I figured I would take it away from him.

He chuckled. "Thief."

I pinched the skin covering his abs and he squirmed.

We sat there for a while and enjoyed the evening breeze. Fall was here and Rosemary was peaceful again. The crowds were gone. Jace's absence still clung to us. We all felt it. We knew we always would. But lately we had all been able to talk about him again. Someone would tell a funny story about him and we would all laugh instead of cry.

Bethy was at work again but Woods still wasn't ready to speak to her. He knew he was wrong. He admitted it to me one night. But he said he couldn't forgive her. I let it go. I knew he just needed more time.

Tripp was also back in town. He had been gone for about a week and packed up his place in South Carolina. Then he'd moved back here into his condo. Woods had given him a place on the board of directors at the club.

"Della?"

"Yes?"

"Do you believe in fate?"

I thought about it a minute. I wasn't sure. I hadn't given much thought to the idea of fate before.

"What exactly do you mean by that?" I asked.

"I mean . . . do you think things happen for a reason, and no matter what we do or what we choose they'll happen anyway?"

He was thinking about Jace's death. He didn't want to hate Bethy. But his heart wasn't letting him forgive her because of his love for Jace.

"I think that everyone's life is controlled by a series of events. They choose what they want and if it is in their control they can reach it. Sometimes luck shines on them and sometimes it doesn't. I also think accidents happen and we are placed in situations where we have to do things for those we love that we don't want to do."

Woods didn't say anything.

I let him think about it. I wasn't going to push him to forgive Bethy.

That would be something he'd have to find within himself when he was ready.

Woods

I slipped my phone in my pocket and waited by my truck for Della's car to pull into the gas station. I had made sure her tank was low before I left the house an hour ago. She was going to need gas before she met me at the Mexican restaurant where we'd gone before our one-night stand. I had convinced her earlier that she wanted the quesadillas for dinner. Talking about melted cheese had been all I needed to get her to agree to drive the short distance out of town.

Her car turned the corner, and just like I'd planned she pulled up to the tank. She had already spotted my truck parked on the other side of the pump when she pulled up.

Her car door swung open and she was grinning at me like I was crazy.

"What are you doing here? I thought you were waiting on me at the restaurant."

I stepped around the pump and leaned against her car. "I believe we've been here before," I said, watching as she realized what I was talking about.

Her smile grew and her eyes twinkled with laughter. "Yes, I believe we have. But good news: this time I can pump my own gas," she said.

I had met her for the first time in this very spot. She'd been wearing tiny little shorts, looking sexy as hell, and had no idea how to pump gas. I had needed a distraction from my life and there she was.

"Damn, I was hoping I could pump it for you," I said.

She pressed her lips together in a smile and shrugged. "If you really want to, then you can."

"I need you to pop the door," I told her, pointing to the little door where the fuel went.

"Oh! I saw you and forgot to do that." I watched as she turned around and bent inside the car to push the button.

I reached into my pocket and pulled out the small box that I had kept hidden in my sock drawer for a week. Della turned around and started to say something but stopped when I went down on one knee.

"A year ago I was lost. My life was a fucked-up mess. I stopped to get gas right here and found this gorgeous brunette who couldn't pump her gas. I then somehow convinced her to eat with me. She made me laugh and made me horny as hell. When the night was over and I had to leave her sleeping on that bed in the hotel, it was hard. I didn't want to. But my life was fucked and she was traveling the world, finding herself."

I stopped as Della reached up and wiped a tear that was running down her face. Her big blue eyes were swimming with tears.

"Then she came back into my life and saved me from hell. She changed my world. She taught me to love and she owns my soul."

Della's small hand went up to cover her mouth and a sob came out.

"Della Sloane, will you marry me?"

She was nodding before I could get the words out of my mouth. I stood up and slipped the diamond that I'd spent weeks trying to find onto her finger. When I found it I had known it was the one. It was worthy enough to grace Della's hand.

"Yes," she finally said before throwing her arms around my neck. "Yes, yes, yes," she chanted, clinging to me.

I held her against me and realized that if there was no such thing as fate, then someone had to be up there dealing out winning hands.

"Can we skip the Mexican and go back to that hotel room instead?" I asked her.

She tilted her head back and flashed me a saucy smile. "What about your truck? I don't want to skip that part."

Neither did I.

Read on for a sneak peek at the next novel

by Abbi Glines set in the world

of Rosemary Beach

Take a Chance

The first book about Grant and Harlow

Available from Atria Books in February 2014

Grant

Why was I here? What was the fucking purpose? Had I gotten this bad? Really? In the past, I'd been able to shake her loose and walk away. Nanette had been my go-to fuck for years, but then she'd gotten needy. And I'd liked it. Somehow, she had managed to get under my skin. I had wanted to be wanted—I was that pathetic. My dad rarely called me; my mom had decided she preferred French models over me years ago.

I was screwed the hell up.

It was time I let this go. Nan had needed me for a time when she felt like she was losing Rush, her brother and safe place, to his new life with his wife and child. Not that Rush wouldn't welcome her with open arms—it was just that she was such a bitch. All she had to do was accept Rush's wife, Blaire. That was it. But the stubborn woman wouldn't do it.

Mine had been the arms she'd run into, and like a fool I had opened them up for her. Now, all I had was a lot of damn drama and a slightly damaged heart. She hadn't claimed it. Not completely. But she had touched a place no one else had. She had needed me. No one had ever needed me. It had made me weak.

To prove my point, here I sat in Nan's father's home, looking for her, waiting on her. She was running wild again, and Rush wasn't coming to the rescue. He had hung up his Superman cape and decided his days of coming to Nan's side were over. I had wanted that. As sick as it was, I had wanted to be her hero. Damn, I was a pussy.

"Drink, kid. Fuck knows you need it," Kiro, Nan's father, said as he shoved a half-empty bottle of tequila into my hands. Kiro was the lead singer of the most legendary rock band in the world. Slacker Demon had been around for twenty years, and their songs still skyrocketed to number one whenever they released a new album.

I started to argue but changed my mind. He was right. I needed a drink. I didn't think about where the dude's mouth had been when I touched the rim of the bottle to my lips and tipped it back.

"You're a smart boy, Grant. What I can't figure is why the hell you're putting up with Nan's shit," Kiro said as he sank down onto the white leather sofa across from me. He was in a pair of black skinny jeans and a silver shirt, unbuttoned and hanging open. Tattoos covered his chest and arms. Women still went crazy over him. It wasn't his looks. He was too damn skinny. A diet of alcohol and drugs would do that to you. But he was Kiro. That was all that mattered to them.

"You gonna ignore me? Hell, she's my daughter and I can't put up with her. Damn crazy bitch, just like her momma," he drawled before taking a pull off a joint.

"That's enough, Daddy." The musical voice that was finding its way into my fantasies lately floated from the doorway.

"There's my baby girl. She's come out of her room to visit,"

Kiro said, grinning at the daughter he actually loved. The one he hadn't abandoned. Harlow Manning was breathtaking. She didn't look like a rock star's kid. She looked like an innocent, sweet country girl, with long, dark hair and eyes that made you forget your fucking name.

"I was going to see if you planned on eating dinner at home tonight or if you were going out," she said. I watched as she stepped into the room and purposely ignored me. That only made me smile.

She didn't like me. I had met her at Rush and Blaire's engagement party and then spoken to her at their wedding reception. Both times hadn't ended well.

"I was thinkin' of going out. I need to party a little. I've stayed inside this house too damn long."

"Oh, okay," she said in that soft voice that I swear was intoxicating.

Kiro frowned. "You lonely? Locking yourself away in that room with your books getting to you, baby girl?"

I couldn't take my eyes off Harlow. She rarely came around when I was here. Nan wasn't exactly kind to her. I got why she didn't like Harlow. She was eaten up with jealousy where Harlow was concerned. Even if it wasn't Harlow's fault that Kiro loved her and didn't seem to give a shit about Nan.

"No, I'm fine. I was just going to wait and eat with you if you planned to eat here. If not, I'll just eat a sandwich in my room."

Kiro started shaking his head. "I don't like that. You're in there too much. I want you to stop reading for tonight. Grant is here and he needs some company. He's a good guy. Talk to him. You can have dinner together while he waits for Nan to return."

Harlow stiffened and finally glanced my way, but only for a moment. "I don't think so."

"Come on, don't be a snob. Grant's a family friend. He's Rush's brother. Have dinner with him."

Harlow's spine stiffened even straighter. She went back to not making eye contact with me. "He's not Rush's brother. If he were, it would be even more disgusting that he's sleeping with Nan."

Kiro grinned as if Harlow was the funniest person in the world and he was proud of her spunk. "My kitten has claws, and apparently only you bring them out. Sleeping with the evil sister has put you on my baby girl's shit list. Now, that's funny as hell." He looked extremely amused as he took another long draw from his joint.

I wasn't amused. I didn't like the fact that Harlow hated me. I wasn't sure how the hell to fix it, though. Turning my back on Nan wasn't possible. She wouldn't be able to handle someone else dropping her. Even if her slutty ass deserved it. I wouldn't let myself think about the boy band she was currently sleeping with. Guess I was wrong about those guys. I thought for sure they were sleeping with each other. Instead, they were all sleeping with Nan.

"Have a good night, Daddy," Harlow said, then turned and walked out of the room before Kiro could demand she stay with me.

Kiro laid his head back and closed his eyes. "Shame she hates you. She's special. Only known one other like her, and it was her mom. Woman stole my heart. I adored her. Worshipped the fucking ground she walked on. I would have thrown all this shit away for her. I had planned on it. I just wanted to wake up each morning and see her there beside me. I wanted to watch her with our baby girl and know that they were mine. But God wanted her more. Took her the fuck away from me. I won't ever get over it. Never."

This wasn't the first time I had heard him ramble on about Harlow's mother. He did it whenever he got high. She was the first thing that came to his mind. I hadn't known that kind of love. Scared the shit out of me, though. I wasn't sure I ever wanted to know it. Kiro had never recovered. I had met the man when I was a kid and my dad had married Rush's mom. Rush had begged his dad, Dean Finlay, the drummer for Slacker Demon, to take me with them on one of his weekend visits.

I had been in awe. It had been the first of many weekends. And Kiro would always talk about "her" and curse God for taking her. It had fascinated me, even as a child. I had never witnessed that kind of devotion.

Even after my dad's short marriage to Rush's mother, Georgianna, I had remained close to Rush. His dad still came to pick me up sometimes when he got Rush. I had grown up personally knowing the most legendary rock band in the world.

"Nan hates her. Who the hell can hate Harlow? She's too damn sweet to hate. Girl hasn't done anything to Nan, yet Nan's mean as a goddamn snake. Poor Harlow stays away from her. I hate to see my baby girl so defenseless. She needs to toughen up. She needs a friend." Kiro set his joint down in an ashtray and turned his head to look at me. "Be her friend, kid. She needs one."

I wanted to be a lot more than Harlow Manning's friend. But she wouldn't even look at me. "Not sure I can be her friend and Nan's at the same time."

Kiro frowned, then sat up and leaned forward. "Three kinds of women in this world. The kind that suck you dry and leave you with nothing. The kind that only want a good time. And the kind that make life worth a damn. That last kind . ... the right woman's the one who gives as much as she takes, and you can't get enough. She's the kind . . . if you lose her, you lose yourself."

His bloodshot eyes told me he hadn't just smoked a joint today. But even high, he made sense. If anyone knew about women, it was Kiro Manning.

"I've had all three. Wish like hell I'd stayed away from the first. The second is all I touch anymore. But that third one . . . I won't ever be the same. And I wouldn't take back one minute I had with Harlow's mom."

He ran his hand through his stringy hair. "Nannette, she's the first kind. Be careful of the first kind. They will fuck you over and walk away laughing."

About the Author

Abbi Glines is the *New York Times*, *USA Today*, and *Wall Street Journal* bestselling author of *Twisted Perfection* and *Simple Perfection*, in addition to several new adult and young adult novels. A devoted booklover, Abbi lives with her family in Alabama. She maintains a Twitter addiction at @AbbiGlines and can also be found at facebook.com/AbbiGlinesAuthor and AbbiGlines.com.

Can't get enough of ABBI GLINES?

You've fallen for the playboys of **Rosemary Beach**. Now, get to know the heartthrobs of **Sea Breeze** in the young adult series that put Abbi Glines on the map.

Available in trade paperback from **Simon Pulse.**